TEMPTED BY HER ISLAND MILLIONAIRE

NINA SINGH

MILLS & BOON

First published in Great Britain 2018
by Mills & Boon, an imprint of HarperCollins*Publishers*
1 London Bridge Street, London, SE1 9GF

Large Print edition 2018

© 2018 Nilay Nina Singh

ISBN: 978-0-263-07440-6

MIX
Paper from
responsible sources
FSC
www.fsc.org   FSC® C007454

This book is produced from independently certified FSC™ paper to ensure responsible forest management. For more information visit www.harpercollins.co.uk/green.

Printed and bound in Great Britain
by CPI Group (UK) Ltd, Croydon, CR0 4YY

For my dear husband.

That was quite an impressive anniversary gift, hon.

And for my children.

Thank you for enduring bitter cold atop a volcano,
waiting for a sunrise with me.

TEMPTED BY
HER ISLAND
MILLIONAIRE

CHAPTER ONE

HIS SISTER WAS starting to get on his nerves.

He loved her more than anyone else on this earth, but she had been pushing the boundaries of that love ever since she'd gotten engaged.

Clint held the cell phone to his ear, only partially listening to her latest panic-stricken rant. He knew better than to try and say anything to calm her down. The last time he'd tried that, he'd gotten an earful of colorful curse words streamed through the line that would have made his construction contractors blush.

He understood, or he was trying hard to anyway. She had a lot on her mind with the wedding fast approaching. In fact, his town car was dropping him off at the airport at this very moment on his way to sunny Maui where Lizzie and her fiancé would be tying the knot in a few short days. Only now she had some sort of pressing issue with a last-minute change, something to do with the catering. An issue she seemed to be taking way out of proportion. He'd simply learn who he had to pay to fix it once he got there. What was one more expense when it came to this wedding? He'd be sure to take care of it after arrival. Again, he wasn't going to tell her that. Right now, Lizzie just needed to vent.

His sister had always been a bit overly dramatic. But this wedding was taking that penchant to a whole new level and making him wonder, for that matter, exactly how many women had been put on this earth simply to irritate him?

"Anyway, how are you doing? Anything new?" Lizzie surprised him by asking. Rant over somehow. Not that he wasn't grateful.

Did he dare tell her? That he was unexpectedly attending her wedding solo since the huge fallout with Maxine the other day. After she'd finally made one ultimatum too many.

He decided not to risk it. Lizzie would no doubt want the distraction and try to probe for all the details. Not something he wanted to get into right now. He'd tell her once he arrived at the resort.

"I'm doing fine," he answered honestly. In truth, it was a relief to have finally severed the relationship with the up-and-coming actress. Maxine had grown increasingly demanding and pouty over the past several months. The only frustration now was that he'd already paid for all her flights, excursions and accommodations. Not to mention a hefty spa-and-beauty package at the resort. Shameful waste. Though part of him couldn't help but wonder if it was worth it. "About to go check in for my flight as a matter of fact."

"I'll let you go then, big brother." She paused but didn't hang up. He knew what was coming and he appreciated it. But it still made him uneasy every time she did it. "And you know how much it means that you're doing all this for me," she said, her voice nearly breaking. "I mean it. Thank you."

So unnecessary. She was the only family he had. He'd been solely responsible for her since they were both barely teens, so of course, he would take care of her wedding. And anything else that would make up for the unfair lot they'd been dealt growing up. She didn't need to thank him for that. The wedding was just one more thing he considered his duty.

Unfortunately, so was having to listen to her mini breakdowns every time a snag occurred.

"You're welcome, Lizzie," he answered simply, then disconnected.

The morning didn't get any better after he'd checked in for his flight. With precision, he'd arrived with just enough time to answer any urgent emails and go over a new bid, then comfortably board without having to rush. The airline announced a delay before he'd even gotten a chance to pull his tablet out and log on to his company intranet.

Clint cursed under his breath. An hour, at least. As luck would have it, his private jet was being serviced. The timing was beyond inconvenient. Well, he wasn't going to sit here in this loud, crowded gate area. He'd go kill the time at the private executive suite the airport provided for certain clientele. Maybe he'd even get a chance to read a paper in some peace and quiet.

He swiped his card to get past the secure glass door to the exclusive suite and realized quickly that peace and quiet were not in the equation this morning.

This was, without question, one of the most embarrassing experiences of her whole life. Rita wanted to sink into the ground as she stammered to answer the airport employee who was very politely and professionally interrogating her. Not only had the other three people in the suite started to stare, she noticed from the corner of her vision that someone else had just walked in—a tall dark man with a leather briefcase. Wonderful. Yet one more person to witness her abject humiliation.

"I'm terribly sorry, miss. But there's no record of anyone sponsoring you to be in this room," the well-heeled, highly polished attendant repeated. Sheila, according to the gold name tag on her uniform. "I'm afraid you'll have to pay for your breakfast and then leave."

"Oh, um… I don't understand… I was told by my friend who's a member that I'd be allowed to hang out here if I wanted, and the flight was delayed. I just thought—" Her words were an incoherent mess. She'd never been good under pressure. And this haughty woman was making her feel like a piece of mud she was trying to brush off her Louboutins.

The attendant remained silent. Rita couldn't detect one iota of sympathy in her eyes.

Oh, what the hell. The mushroom omelet and mimosa weren't worth the trouble. Though it had to be the most delicious breakfast she'd ever been served.

"Fine, what do I owe you for the breakfast?"
She reached for her wallet.

"With the drink, it will be seventy-five dollars."

She nearly dropped her purse when she heard
the figure. "Seventy-five dollars?" How could
that be? Had they personally flown in the mush-
rooms straight from Japan and had a master chef
prepare the meal?

Sheila merely nodded in such a superior way
that Rita knew she wasn't imagining her satisfied
smirk of a smile. Satisfaction at her discomfort.

Currently between jobs, Rita had been trying
hard to maintain a certain budget. A tight one.
The loss of that kind of money had tears spring-
ing into her eyes. With shaky fingers, she reached
for her credit card, which was already perilously
close to the limit as she was about to spend a
week in Hawaii. Most of her expenses were taken
care of by the wedding party, but she'd still need
money for extra meals or souvenirs. Why had she
ever walked in here?

Suddenly, a wall in the form of a navy-blue
silk shirt appeared in her vision. Someone had
stepped between her and the employee, his back
to Rita. The newcomer who'd walked in about

thirty seconds ago. "Excuse me to interrupt, here. But I'd like to sponsor the young lady as my guest. Please put her breakfast charges on my account."

What?

Great. Now she was getting pity charity from strangers who wanted to pay for her breakfast. "That won't be necessary," she argued to the man's back. Lord, he was broad shouldered. She could see his toned muscles outlined under the finely tailored shirt. It was difficult to get around him to address the attendant.

"I insist," the stranger said to her over his shoulder.

"Certainly, sir. How nice to see you again," the attendant said to him. Rita dared a peek over his shoulder to look at her. It appeared that now Sheila was the one who looked somewhat uncomfortable, she noted with no small degree of satisfaction herself.

Still, she couldn't have random strangers pay for her breakfast. "I said that won't be necessary." She tried to step around him once more.

The man actually stretched his arm out to block her!

Of all the nerve. Granted, he was trying to do something incredibly nice for her but to actually stop her from having any say in the matter was a bit much. Nice or not, he had no right. It wasn't like she really needed his help. The amount would cause a dent in her bank account but she did have the means to pay it.

But it was too late. Sheila flashed him a bright smile, the smirk entirely gone. "I'll take care of it right away, Mr. Fallon."

Mr. Fallon. He turned to her as the attendant walked away. Rita blinked and did a double take as his deep brown eyes met hers. Recognition dawned with a sinking sensation as she realized exactly who he was—the dark hair, the familiar coloring and features.

"I didn't mean to insult you," he told her. "It's just that I happened to have witnessed that particular employee's pettiness before. I might have to initiate some sort of formal complaint about her with the airport actually."

Oh, no. That wasn't what she wanted at all. "Please don't do that. I don't want to think about someone losing their job because of me."

He quirked an eyebrow in question. "No matter how badly they had it coming?"

She shook her head. "And it's not that I feel insulted."

"No?"

"No, not really." She blew out a breath. "I'm just a bit embarrassed. I wish I'd never walked in here in the first place."

His eyes narrowed on her. Rita couldn't quite read the expression on his face. "I'm actually really glad you did."

A small sensation tingled at the base of her spine. Was he trying to flirt with her now? Yep, definitely the most mortifying thing to ever happen to her. To make the whole thing so much worse, Clinton Fallon had no clue who she was. He didn't even remember her.

Clint wanted to tell the young lady he could relate. It hadn't been that long ago that people like Sheila had talked down to him in the same manner he'd just witnessed her being subjected to. Her embarrassed expression and obviously flustered state when he'd walked in had touched a nerve within him that he'd long since thought was dormant. Apparently, the universe decided he was due for a periodic reminder.

He was glad for it, as he'd just told her. He

didn't want to get too complacent or take anything for granted.

"I guess I owe you a thank-you," she was saying.

Guessed? "Uh...you're welcome."

She reached for her carry-on. "I think I'll leave."

Clint stepped in front of her before she got far. Was she confused? He'd just taken care of the matter so that she could stay. "You no longer have to."

Something flashed behind her eyes. It didn't strike him as gratitude. Far from it. He had offended her. Well, what was he supposed to have done? Let her get tossed out on her behind?

"Nevertheless. I'm not sure I want to stay in here any longer."

"You mentioned your flight was delayed. At least finish your breakfast."

"I'm sure it's cold now," she muttered, then blew out a breath. "I'm sorry. It's just—I've really been looking forward to this trip. And so far it hasn't exactly started off on the most positive note."

"I understand," he told her, a feeling of empathy settling deep within his chest. He did understand. More than she knew.

* * *

Rita adjusted her collar and tried to quell the shaking in her stomach. Clinton Fallon was standing before her without any clue as to who she was. Apparently, she hadn't made much of an impression on him all those years ago when she'd been at university with his sister. First, he'd witnessed her abject humiliation by the suite attendant. And now she was going to have to find a way to introduce herself.

Or reintroduce herself as the case may be. By contrast, she couldn't count the number of times she'd thought about him over the years. As if she hadn't felt silly enough about that small fact until this encounter.

She was trying to figure out a way to tell him exactly who she was when he extended his hand. "I'm Clinton—"

"I know who you are," she blurted out without really thinking.

He blinked. "You do?"

A small lump of disappointment settled in her gut. He really had no inkling, no recollection whatsoever. Why was she surprised? Or even disappointed? People like him didn't take much note of ladies like her.

And exactly what kind of lady was she now? How would she begin to describe herself? Perhaps she could use the term *recent divorcée*. Or *unemployed veterinarian*. Or *failed daughter*. Unfortunately, any one of those could apply.

"Here. Let's give this a try." She removed a hair band from her wrist and quickly tied her thick dark hair in a loose ponytail. Then she removed a pair of thick glasses from her pocket and perched them on her nose.

Clint's only response was a completely blank look. Still nothing.

Rita sighed. Now she was just humiliating herself even more. He had no idea who she was. How often had she thought about him over the years? How often had she wondered where he was and what he was doing?

While he hadn't even given her a second thought, it seemed.

"I went to school with Lizzie," she told him. "You and I met in passing a few times at various school-sponsored family events." She extended her hand. "Rita Paul. I'm actually on my way to your sister's wedding myself."

His smile grew wide as he took it. "I'm sorry. I'm just so bad with faces."

"No need to apologize." Though she did appreciate the effort. An awkward moment passed as they limply shook hands. As if neither could decide who should let go first. Why was she behaving so loopily around this man? Finally, Rita pulled out of his grasp.

"It should have occurred to me that at least one or two of Lizzie's friends would be on this flight," Clint continued. "I'm not used to flying with the airlines. My private aircraft is undergoing some repairs."

"Did you really just say that your jet is in the shop?"

He gave her an embarrassed smile. "I guess I did."

He'd certainly come far. Though again, she wasn't surprised. The man she'd met all those years ago was clearly driven and talented. "You were just starting out in the construction business back when Lizzie and I were in school."

He nodded. "That's correct."

"You've just acquired a company, I believe."

"Correct again. The man I worked for was ready

to retire. Said he trusted me more than anyone else to take over. Gave me quite a deal when he sold me the business."

"A deal you clearly made the most of then took to new astronomical heights."

He studied her. "I guess you could say that. Along with some well-placed investments, things have gone pretty well."

What an understatement. The man owned a private jet. She knew he'd single-handedly put his sister through school. No doubt, he was the one paying for this lavish destination wedding.

Clint Fallon represented the epitome of a self-made success story. She'd followed his life for a while in the local papers and news sites after graduating from school. Everyone was fascinated by a self-made man. But then her own life had gone completely awry. Unlike Clint and his string of successes, she'd only managed to accumulate one failure after another. Though heaven knew he'd been handed a much worse set of circumstances.

Well, this was her chance to get away from all that and try to forget. For the next few days anyway. This trip was all about Lizzie and her future husband and the love they shared.

She was trying to come up with a response when the airline announced they were finally boarding. "I should head out to the lobby," she told him. "I'm seated toward the back. I'll be one of the first they call."

But he reached for her arm to stop her from leaving. "Wait. I happen to know the seat next to me is free."

"But I thought this was a full flight. They were asking for volunteers to give up their spots."

"Fairly recent development. I didn't get a chance to update the airline. I was supposed to be, ah…traveling with someone. Their plans fell through at the last minute."

Understanding dawned. Pictures of Clint always showed him with a female companion. Always someone very glamorous and beautiful. None seemed to last for more than a few news cycles. The timing of his latest breakup appeared fairly inconvenient. He was going stag to his own sister's wedding.

"You can sit with me up in first class."

She had to decline. He'd already done more than enough by paying for her breakfast and vouching for her to stay in the lounge. "I appreciate that. But it's not necessary."

He blinked at her. "I could use the company," he countered, then pulled his phone out of his pocket. "It'll just take me a second."

Before she knew what he was up to, he was quickly on the phone with the airlines. Clearly, he had some kind of executive direct line that reached an employee right away.

Clint wasn't terribly good at reading her frustrated vibe.

He was already ending the call before she could protest any further. "You're all set. We can board together."

Rita clamped down on her annoyance. If she said anything further she would merely sound petulant and ungrateful. Never mind that she was trying to feel more in charge of herself, more in control of her life. This flight had literally been the first travel ticket she'd purchased for herself, paid for completely on her own. And Clint Fallon had just given it away and upgraded her to first class.

She knew it was illogical of her to be angry or to feel slighted. Clint had no idea of her circumstances. Or the silly symbolic meaning she'd put behind the whole trip.

Rita herself had only actually just now realized how much it meant to her.

It appeared Rita had not taken him seriously when he'd said he could use some company on the flight. Despite sitting right next to him, she'd barely spoken two words. The complete opposite of what he knew would have happened with Maxie. She would have no doubt talked his ear off about everything from her latest gig to the spa treatment she'd been scheduled for.

Something between the two extremes would have been nice.

He should have taken the opportunity to get some work done. But he'd found himself distracted by the delicate rose scent of her perfume. Her jet-black hair brushed against his shoulder when she shifted in her seat and he'd had to resist the urge to ask her if he could run his fingers through the thick silky strands.

How uncharacteristic of him.

Now, several hours later, she was just as quiet. They were finally approaching the Grande Maui resort in Kaanapali. And he was experiencing yet another silent ride. The woman had no interest in speaking to him.

The vehicle finally came to a stop and they both exited, then waited as the young driver pulled their bags out of the rear trunk.

He heard Lizzie's excited voice from behind before he could even reach for his luggage.

"You're here!" his sister shouted, her voice breathy with excitement. He found himself bear-hugged in her skinny arms a short second later. She noticed Rita standing next to them when she finally let go. "You're here too." Lizzie glanced at the town car. "You two came together?"

She didn't wait for an answer as she took Rita in her arms next. Clint watched as the two women also embraced, Rita's dark hair and olive skin a complete contrast to his sister's red coloring and fair complexion. There was true affection in their tight hug.

"I ran into Rita at the airport," he answered his sister over their heads.

"Oh, how fortunate," Lizzie exclaimed as they finally pulled apart.

"Yes. Very lucky for me," Rita began. "He paid for my breakfast, saved me from a very embarrassing situation at the executive lounge, then upgraded me to first class."

If she actually felt lucky about any of that, her

tone distinctly said otherwise. Was she mad at him? Whatever for? The thought tugged at him. Usually, the women in his life made it more than clear whatever his transgressions against them might be. Maybe he was interpreting her tiredness after a long flight for sarcasm. Or perhaps he was hearing things; the large gushing stone fountain behind them was pretty loud after all.

"You'll both have to tell me exactly how you ran into each other," Lizzie said and peeked inside the still-waiting car. "But where's Maxie?"

Both ladies turned to him, awaiting his answer. He bit back a curse. This wasn't something he wanted to get into in front of Rita Paul. Though he'd be hard-pressed to say why that was so.

"Change of plans. I'll be unaccompanied on this trip," he told his sister, hoping beyond any real expectation that she'd let the matter drop.

She didn't. Lizzie's eyes grew wide and a huge grin spread across her lips. "I heard nothing of this change."

"Things didn't work out." And that's all he wanted to say on the matter.

His sister's smile grew wider. "You don't say!"

She'd never really taken to Maxie. Not that there'd been anyone he'd been with so far that she'd approved of. His sister kept telling him the women he dated were far too shallow.

Little did Lizzie know, at this point in his life, he wanted shallow. Particularly now, when he was no longer solely responsible for his sister.

Rita glanced from one of them to the other. Suddenly, Lizzie clamped a hand over her mouth; the smile completely disintegrated. "Oh, Rita, I don't mean to be insensitive. I'm so sorry things didn't work out between you and Jay."

A flash of regret seemed to pass through Rita's eyes, but it was gone in an instant. "It wasn't meant to be. Let's just focus on celebrating you and Jonathon."

"I missed you." The two women linked arms, then slowly started to walk toward the front desk. Clint hovered behind, tipping the bell steward who loaded their luggage onto a cart. His gaze remained on Rita as she walked away. He didn't know the woman from a passing acquaintance but he felt... He couldn't even describe what he felt.

He'd met her years ago and had somehow forgotten her. Which seemed unbelievable given his reaction to her now.

She was one of his sister's close friends. A

bridesmaid in her wedding. Based on their conversation just now, she'd clearly just come out of what sounded like a serious relationship.

The last thing he wanted was any kind of meaningful relationship himself. Not for several years. He'd done all he could for his sister. She was a grown, educated, about-to-be-married woman. He intended this next period of his life to be all about his growing business and doing all the things he hadn't been able to do after he and Lizzie had been orphaned when he was merely sixteen. His sister had only been fourteen.

Lizzie turned and gave him a questioning look. He read it as "Hurry up, already." For the younger sibling, she could certainly be quite bossy, Clint thought as he strolled to where they now stood by the check-in desk.

"This is the man whose credit card is covering all these charges," Lizzie told the desk clerk as she pointed at him. "Including the expanded catering menu we discussed earlier."

The gentleman handed him a key card. "Mr. Fallon. Welcome. Your suite is ready and waiting for you. You'll find a chilled bottle of champagne and a basket of fruit."

Lizzie clapped her hands and turned to him.

"Excellent, Rita and I will be snagging that champagne from you, big brother."

"Is that so? And why should I relinquish it to you two?"

Lizzie huffed with impatience, as if the answer should be obvious. "Because us girls are celebrating. More than just my upcoming nuptials."

"Fine. Consider it yours." He knew he could be too indulgent with her sometimes. But this was her wedding. "What else will you two be celebrating then?"

She draped her arm around Rita's shoulders. "We are also celebrating this young lady's newly found freedom."

Rita's eyes flickered downward. She looked far from celebratory at the moment.

Clint signed the paperwork he'd been handed and watched as the two women slowly made their way down the hall.

So who exactly was Jay? And was there any chance Rita was still hung up on him?

But there was no denying the real, much bigger question—why did Clint want to know so badly?

CHAPTER TWO

HER DIVORCE WAS hardly a cause for celebration.
Rita was just getting used to the idea that she
was single again. The breakup had been her idea.
She'd been the one who wanted out of her marriage. Still, it wasn't something she wanted to
party over. Jay hadn't been a bad person. He
hadn't even been a bad husband. In fact, he'd
make someone else a fitting spouse one day. Just
not her.

But Lizzie's heart was in the right place. So
Rita figured she'd drink Clint's champagne with
her. Speaking of, she hadn't missed Clint's curious glance in her direction when Lizzie had spoken of her breakup. Now, as they passed through
the open-air lobby on the way to his suite, she
could feel his intense gaze on her back. The
knowledge sent a tingle of awareness along the
surface of her skin.

Cut it out.

She was simply reacting to seeing her crush

again after all these years. And that's all Clint
had ever been: a crush.

"And it all starts tonight!" Lizzie chimed with
excitement.

Rita was paying just enough attention to know
Lizzie was rambling on about the various sight-
seeing tours and excursions planned for the wedding party. Apparently, it all kicked off with a
traditional Hawaiian luau this evening.

Good thing one of them was talking; God bless
her old friend for never being at a loss for words,
as Rita wasn't feeling particularly chatty. Heaven
knew she hadn't said much to Clint on the plane
ride over. But what would she have talked about?
Her stalled career? Her failed marriage? And she
certainly didn't want to get into her currently
very strained relationship with her parents.

At least she wasn't the only one here alone.
Clint was also without a plus-one. Looked like
they both were leaving some part of their pasts
behind.

They finally reached his door and Clint used
his card to let them in. Rita had to bite down a
gasp as she stepped inside. His suite was the size
of a small apartment. A wall of glass stood opposite them, the view a spectacular one of the

ocean and the island mountain in the distance. Pity the woman who was supposed to be here and was now missing out on all this.

Among the other things she was missing out on.

Rita couldn't help but study Clint as he walked to the veranda and pulled the sliding door open. She'd certainly had good taste all those years ago when she'd first started crushing on the man. Tall and lean, he seemed to be quite fit. And he had the most striking facial features. Where his sister was fair with a patrician nose, Clint had more the look of a well-mixed genealogy. Lizzie had mentioned once that there was some Asian blood in their family ancestry. Though those genes hadn't found his sister, Clint clearly had what would be described as such characteristics. Overall, it made for a dashing, exotic look that definitely made him stand out in a crowd.

"They gave you the good stuff," Lizzie said as she pulled a green glass bottle out of the ice bucket.

"And I'm giving it to you two," Clint replied.

"I suppose we can let you have a glass. Not a big one though." Lizzie pinched her fingers in a demonstration of how much his pour would be.

"We probably shouldn't have too much right now anyway. There'll be plenty of food and drink at the luau later this evening," she said, then glanced at Rita as if looking for agreement.

"Right."

"By the way—" Lizzie addressed her brother "—Tessa Campbell has been asking about you since she arrived. She happens to be your roommate, Rita."

Clint gave her a distracted nod as he stood staring at the majestic view in front of them. "Which one was she again?"

Lizzie gave an exaggerated roll of her eyes in Rita's direction, the effect so comical it made her giggle. "How can you not remember?" she asked her brother as she gave him the bottle to uncork. "She's been hitting on you since the tenth grade. Wait till she finds out you're here alone."

He actually groaned. "Now I remember. What are the chances I'll be able to avoid her?"

"Slim to none," his sister replied. "She is a member of the wedding party after all."

"Great."

Clint's tone held every hint of resignation. He was a man used to such attention. She wasn't surprised. It was all merely an annoyance for him. He deftly uncorked the bottle with a pop and grabbed two flutes off the serving table then began pouring. Tiny florescent bubbles floated through the air. He handed each of them a glass.

Lizzie suddenly let out a laugh that had her snorting bubbly champagne through her nose. The sight, in turn, made Rita laugh.

"What's so funny?" Clint wanted to know.

Lizzie rubbed the tip of her nose. "I just had an image of you ducking behind palm trees during the luau when you saw Tessa approaching."

Rita laughed harder at the visual that invoked. Clint glanced from one to the other, a resigned expression on his face. "I'm glad you two find this so amusing."

"I'm sorry," Rita told him but she couldn't seem to stop one last giggle. When was the last time she'd really laughed? The past few months had been an emotional hailstorm. She was so glad to be here, finally able to get away. To have it be for such a happy occasion was just icing on the cake. This chance to step back from her troubles for a while was exactly what she needed right now.

But then Clint focused those dark chestnut-brown eyes on her, his lips curved into a smile.

She had to suck in a breath just as her stomach did a dive straight to her toes. Perhaps she'd found trouble yet again.

Clint's intention to get some rest before the luau with a quick nap was not going well. Every time he started to drift off, a set of dark brown eyes framed by silky jet-black hair sprang into his mind's eye and jolted him awake. What was wrong with him?

He was simply here to see his sister married off and to give her away. Not to explore a wayward attraction to a friend of hers.

A glance at the wall clock across the room told him the shuttle to take them into town for tonight's festivities would be arriving right about now. He had to get going. Lizzie didn't tolerate lateness. Not even from the big brother who was paying for this whole shindig. He didn't mind. Somehow his sister had escaped the cynicism spouted by their grandmother all those years. Bless her for it.

Maybe Lizzie would prove him and his grandmother wrong and make her marriage work. Maybe she'd be the one to break the Fallon chain of doomed relationships.

Lord knew, he wasn't going to be the one to try. If that made him cynical, so be it. At least Lizzie had found love. Or what she thought was love. But then she'd always been the dreamer. While he'd had to be the responsible, serious one. He'd had no choice. With both parents gone and only an elderly, bitter matron in charge of them, the burden of responsibility had fallen solely on his shoulders.

He figured he'd done okay. They both had, he and his sister. Hokey as it sounded, he'd have to say he was proud of the woman his sister had become. And happy for her that she'd found someone. Jonathon was a good man. He'd make Lizzie a good husband. Someday, he'd make a good father.

Not that Clint was in any kind of hurry to become an uncle, he mused as he walked to the bathroom and turned on the shower. It would have to be a short one. Officially, Clint was the main host of this wedding. He couldn't be missing shuttles and ending up running late to the events. That also meant he had to be very cordial and very polite to every one of their guests.

So it galled him that there was only one in particular he was thinking of right now, wondering if they'd be seated anywhere near each other. Or maybe even together. He didn't know the full wedding party details; he had left Lizzie and Jonathon pretty much to their own devices when it came to planning.

Now he wished he'd been more involved. It might have avoided the whole fiasco at the airport when he couldn't even remember who Rita was. That had been wildly embarrassing. Had he apologized to her? He couldn't recall. If he didn't run into her tonight, he'd have to make it a point to find her and do so.

Right. And that would be the only reason for him to want to seek her out.

Damn it. Why couldn't he stop thinking about her?

Shutting off the water and toweling off, Clint realized he barely had time to make it downstairs in time for the shuttle bus. Throwing on a pair of khaki shorts and a Hawaiian shirt, he didn't bother to button it as he ran toward the hallway stairs that led to the lobby. Waiting for the elevator would be too risky.

In his hurry, Clint realized too late that someone else was on the stairway making their way down. The crash was unavoidable. Unable to stop himself at the speed he was going, he collided hard with an unsuspecting, soft body. He just barely managed to catch her in his arms and avoid what was sure to be a harrowing tumble down several sets of steps.

Turned out he wouldn't have to go looking for Rita after all.

"Oh, my—" Her words cut off as chocolate-brown eyes blinked at him with shock. Her gaze drooped down to his bare chest for a split second before snapping back up to his face.

"I'm so sorry," he began. "Are you all right?"

She blinked once more. "You're not even dressed."

Clint made himself release her in order to pull his shirt together. He began hastily buttoning. "Yeah, part of the reason for my rush. I'm running a little late."

"I guess *running* would be the operative word."

"And *colliding*. Don't forget *colliding*. You never answered my question."

"Question?"

"Are you all right? I didn't hurt you, did I?"

"I'm fine, just a little startled." She adjusted the hem of her sundress, which had shifted somewhat as a result of their collision. And what a pretty dress it was, a shiny number with thin straps that rested delicately on her toned shoulders. The navy blue of the fabric brought out the deep, rich hue of her silky, smooth skin.

Had he ever noticed a woman's dress before? Or how it brought out the color of her skin?

"I'm really sorry, Rita." To think, he'd intended earlier to apologize to her for something completely different: forgetting who she was. His mea culpas when it came to her were accumulating.

"Why are you taking the stairs?" he asked her. "Aren't you on a much higher floor?"

She shrugged. "I always take the stairs. It's better for you."

Well, she certainly was fit. And that dress made no bare bones about it. It showed off her long, toned legs and narrow waist.

This was getting ridiculous. He'd nearly caused her to wipe out down the stairs for heaven's sake. Not to mention he'd hauled her against his bare chest to keep her from falling. And now he couldn't stop ogling her. In a deserted stairway, no less.

"We should probably get down there," he said and motioned for her to go ahead down the final flight of steps. As he followed, he forced himself not to look at her shapely, rounded behind. Though it wasn't easy.

There was a whole pig twisting around on a spit. Head and hooves and all. Rita couldn't bear to look at the sight another second. She wasn't a strict vegetarian by any means. But her profession as a veterinarian made such a scene difficult to watch. In fact, she felt a bit queasy.

The rest of the crowd stood next to the open fire pit, oohing and aahing at the large animal about to be served as their dinner. A crowd that included the entire wedding party. She walked toward the water, away from the buffet area where the rest of the feast was being set up.

The party faced the sea, with a majestic view of the mountains on one side and crystal-blue water as far as the eye could see on the other. Banana-leaf-covered cabanas surrounded a large stage area in the center. Tables and tables of various dishes were already being set up.

Clint Fallon had spared no expense for his sister's wedding. Rita nudged the sand at her feet with her sandaled toe. She glanced over to where he stood with the rest of the crowd. Lizzie had been right about Tessa Campbell wanting to corner him. The woman had made a beeline to Clint's side as soon as they'd exited the shuttle bus. She'd been within two feet of him ever since. Several times, when Rita had ventured to look their way, Tessa had her hand on his arm or his shoulder. She'd definitely dominated his full attention so far.

Though Rita got the distinct feeling Clint was merely being polite. Actually, Clint looked somewhat uncomfortable with the constant touching.

Not that it would bother her if there was anything more than that developing between them. And the frustration she felt at that thought wasn't something she was going to dwell on. She thought of their near disaster on the stairs earlier. Like she'd fallen against a hard wall of pure male. She rubbed her cheek where it had landed against his bare chest when he'd barreled into her. Lord, he'd felt solid.

"Thought you'd taken off." A masculine voice sounded behind her and made her jump. Clint. Rita turned to find him no more than a few feet behind her, as if her thoughts had conjured him.

"Just wanted to admire the water for a bit."

He came to stand beside her, both of them facing the coastline. "You find it a much more palatable view than the one back there over by the fire pit."

He was an observant one. "Yes, well, there's that too." He must have been watching her. So maybe Tessa didn't have so much of his attention after all. "Was it that obvious?"

He smiled. "Your disdain was clear."

Oh, no. She hoped she wasn't coming off in that way. As if she were turning her nose up at the chosen venue or choice of entertainment. Sometimes her shyness was known to come off as a haughtiness. It had gotten her into trouble more than once. "It's just that when you spend your days taking care of animals, seeing one spinning above a fire pit that way is a little off-putting."

Something shifted behind Clint's eyes. Then he actually thwacked himself in the forehead with the palm of his hand. "It's you!"

"I beg your pardon?"

"Sarita. With the neon purple hair. Lizzie's roommate off and on during her school days. You were studying to be a veterinarian."

Ah, so now he was finally remembering. Took him long enough. "Wow, that didn't take you long at all," she said, her voice dripping with sarcasm.

He had the decency to duck his head as if chagrined. "I've been meaning to apologize for that." He spread his hands. "But you gotta cut me some slack. You never looked the same those few times I saw you. I mean, was your hair ever the same color?"

She had to give him that. Her puny attempts at college-girl rebellion centered around changing her hair constantly. Her father absolutely hated it. Which was the point, wasn't it? Still, Clint could have registered some recognition before now.

"And Rita's not your name," he declared. "That threw me off too."

"It's a shortened version of my name. As is yours."

He pursed his lips, as if that thought hadn't occurred to him. "I suppose you're right."

He supposed? Of course, she was right. Clint was short for Clinton. How was that any different than shortening Sarita to Rita? She didn't get a chance to ask as they were interrupted.

"There you are! I lost track of you." Tessa ran up to Clint and wagged her finger at him.

Clint actually groaned out loud. Tessa didn't notice. Or she didn't really care. Then he shocked her by placing both his hands around Rita's waist.

That Tessa definitely noticed. Her eyes grew wide with shock. And annoyance.

"I was just looking for Sarita. We ran into each other at the airport and I've been meaning to catch up with her ever since."

He was? Or was he just trying to use her to deflect Tessa's attentions? She wasn't sure how she felt about that last possibility. But when she glanced his way, his eyes implored her to go along.

His expression was so desperate, she almost felt sorry for him for a split second. "Yes, I'm hoping to hear about what Clint's been up to all these years since we've last seen each other."

Tessa would not be deterred. She crooked her hand into Clint's elbow. "Well, we can't have you two off by yourselves. This is a party after all."

"You know, you're absolutely right," Clint agreed with a wide smile that almost seemed genuine, even as he gently pulled his arm free. "We'll just be another minute."

Tessa's face fell. It was the first time Rita had actually observed such a physical embodiment of that expression. Tessa cleared her throat. "All right then. Don't take too long," she added before walking away.

"Very smooth, Mr. Fallon."

"What do you mean?"

"I mean the way you dismissed her while somehow agreeing with her. Very, very smooth."

"I told her the truth. I really do want to hear more about you. What better time than tonight? In this wonderful setting?"

She couldn't read too much into that comment. "Now that you finally remember who I am?"

He started to object but then apparently thought better of it. "And yes, I could use a break from Tessa, sweet as she is. Just stay by my side throughout the night and maybe she'll leave me alone."

"So I'm supposed to let you utilize our newly rediscovered friendship to allow you to avoid a potential suitor?"

He grabbed his chest in mock outrage. "That's only the secondary motive, remember?"

"Why?"

"Why what?"

"Why would I agree to do that?"

He quirked an eyebrow. "Because you can't resist my charm?"

Rita gave him a thumbs-down. "Try again."

"Because you've taken pity on me?"

This time she shook her head.

"Come on," he pleaded. "Just for tonight. So that I can maybe relax and enjoy this amazing dinner and the traditional performance."

She supposed he did at least have a right to that. Given that it was his sister's wedding they were all here for. Besides, she'd been thankful to Clint so many times in the past. Like when he'd bought his sister the car they'd both used to get from their off-campus dorm to their classes in the dead of winter. Or during junior year when their preferred choice of housing had fallen through and he'd pulled all sorts of strings to get them a place to stay.

Just admit that the prospect of spending the evening with him isn't exactly a turnoff.

She gave him a nonchalant shrug. "Why not?"

Somehow, against her better judgment, she'd just agreed to spend the evening close by Clint's side.

"I take it you won't be indulging in the main course," Clint said as he escorted Rita toward the numerous buffet tables laden with island food. So far, she was being a good sport about their earlier agreement to help him keep Tessa at bay. She'd stayed by his side and made sure to keep the conversation going between the two of them. Just generally staying in his company which he was enjoying way more than he should.

Truth be told, he hadn't been expecting to get much pleasure out of this evening. He wasn't exactly a luau type. Thanks to Rita, however, the evening was so far turning out quite differently than he'd imagined. In a very pleasant way.

The way the other woman was shooting daggers at him from across the serving area made it clear she'd noticed the camaraderie between them.

"You would be correct," Rita responded as they reached the first table.

Sarita. No wonder he hadn't recognized her. He could hardly be faulted for not realizing at first glance that she was the bespectacled, purple-haired, shy girl he'd see occasionally when he visited Lizzie at school. Hard to believe this was the same woman standing before him now.

"It's not like I'll go hungry," she added, breaking into his thoughts and motioning to the massive number of dishes laid out before them. He didn't even recognize half the plates. Tropical fruit, various pulled meats, grilled vegetables. In the center of every table sat a bowling-ball-sized bowl of some kind of pinkish pudding-like substance.

"Any idea what that is?" he asked her.

"I believe it's what's known as poi."

"Pa—what, now?"

She laughed as she handed him an empty plate, then grabbed one for herself. "Based on some reading I've done, it's made from some kind of native plant. It's supposed to be full of essential vitamins and minerals. It's supposed to be very good for you. Particularly for—" she paused mid-sentence "—um… Never mind."

Judging by the way she suddenly ducked her head, something had clearly made her uncomfortable.

"What were you going to say?"

"Nothing. Just an article I read."

"I'm a little hurt that you aren't willing to educate me. Perfectly okay that I'll remain woefully ignorant about whatever this *pwah* is."

She granted him a small laugh. "Poi. It's just very popular with the men in particular."

"Yeah, why's that?"

They both reached for the same serving spoon and the brush of her fingers against his sent a spark of awareness down to his center. Suddenly, he realized what she was referring to. The poi must be considered to lend some kind of boost to male performance.

She quickly pulled her hand away.

"I think I figured it out." He reached for the next item. "Not that someone like me would be concerned about that."

Why the hell had he just said that?

Damn it, now the air between them was awkward and strained. When they'd been having such a relaxed conversation earlier.

"That was just a joke," he said by way of explanation.

"Does that mean it's not true? That you could perhaps use the poi?"

"What? No! I mean, yes. I mean, of course it's true." Saints above. It was like he didn't even know how to speak around this woman.

She popped a pineapple chunk into her mouth and winked at him with bemusement. He had to remind himself to breathe.

"Ha, ha."

Just to be funny, he scooped a ridiculous amount of the poi and dropped it in the center of his plate.

The show was just starting as they took their

seats. He stole a glance at Rita next to him as she watched. She seemed thoroughly entranced by the story the performers were enacting on the stage. Tales about native islanders leaving their home to find more hospitable islands. Kings and queens leading their people to new lands, the culture and customs that they brought with them and how they mixed with inhabitants already living there.

Rita looked like she could be one of those queens. Or a regal princess adjusting to life on a new island. Her sundress swayed softly in the breeze. The glow of the lit torches brought out the dark golden specks of her eyes. Rather than wearing the flower lei they'd received upon arrival around her neck, she'd loosely wrapped it around the crown of her head. The overall effect was mesmerizing.

So much so that Clint barely noticed when the story depiction part of the show was over and the hula dancing had begun. Rhythmic drums filled the air as the dancers bounced to the music, their hips moving in ways that seemed to defy anatomical possibility. The dancers then formed a circle around the tables. Lizzie and Jonathon sat at the table next to them. The woman onstage spoke into her microphone. "I understand there are a bride and groom here celebrating with us."

One of the dancers extended a hand to Lizzie, who took it and then stood from the table. Jonathon stood as well with another dancer leading him by the elbow. All four started making their way toward the stage. Various other couples in the dining area were similarly led.

"Please come participate with us in a traditional celebratory dance," the woman said into the mic.

On her way to the stage, Lizzie suddenly stopped behind him. "Come on, big brother. I don't want you to miss out on this." She grabbed him by the crook of the elbow and pulled.

"Oh, no, you don't. I am not a dancer."

"Tonight you are." She tugged on his arm until he had no choice but to stand.

His sister wanted him to dance. Onstage. A traditional Hawaiian hula. Well, he wasn't going down alone.

"Rita? Care to join us?"

Her jaw fell. "Uh… I'll sit this one out."

"Come on. Don't make me suffer this alone." Before he could finish the sentence, the female dancer behind him took Rita by the hand and made her stand. Essentially making the decision for her. Clint decided he'd be forever indebted to the woman. They made their way toward the stage.

Once there, he found himself thrust in Rita's direction as everyone coupled up to dance, the women in front of the men. A dancer in the front led them, instructing how to move the hips just so. Rita did as instructed. And she seemed to have quite a knack for it. Her hips moved in swift circles in front of him and he thought perhaps his lungs would stop functioning.

Sweet heavens, perhaps he shouldn't have had any of the poi. Not that it would have made any kind of difference.

The early-morning jog along the beach was supposed to clear his head. But images from the previous evening kept invading Clint's mind as he ran at a punishing pace along the water. Rita's smile as she was teasing him about the local delicacy. The way she'd tried to avoid looking at the main dish.

How her hips had moved as she danced in front of him.

So he thought he must have been imaging it when he looked toward the horizon and saw her in the water climbing onto a surfboard, assisted by a tan, blond man. She appeared to be taking a surfing lesson. The man grabbed her about the waist as he held her steady on the waves.

How many times last night had his fingers itched to do the same thing? He couldn't count the number of times he'd awoken after midnight from a dream that prominently featured a dark-haired beauty with a flower lei adorning her head.

He watched her laugh as she toppled off the board and splashed in the water once more. The instructor immediately grabbed her and assisted her back on. Clint suddenly felt an irrationally intense dislike for the man.

This had to stop. He couldn't be having these thoughts. About her or anyone else. He didn't need any kind of disruption in his life right now. Didn't have time for it. He certainly didn't have the time or the inclination for a serious relation-ship with anyone, let alone a woman like Rita. She deserved nothing less than total commit-ment. Something he wasn't sure he'd ever be willing to give.

Good thing there were no group activities planned for today. He could use the time to clear his head. The next outing on the agenda wasn't until after midnight tonight, when they'd be picked up to go to Haleakala to see the sunrise atop the volcanic crater. He'd be sure to steer clear of her then.

You Fallon men have no idea how to fall in love without completely sacrificing your souls.

His grandmother was right. Not that he had any kind of notion that he was falling for Rita. It was simply the romantic mood of this wedding and the sensuous setting of the tropical island. Still, he would have to make sure not to let silly whims get the better of him from now on. Asking Rita to pretend they were interested in getting to know each other better had been a mistake. He would have been better off just dodging Tessa's advances.

Much better off than what he was feeling now.

CHAPTER THREE

IF HER TEETH chattered any harder, Rita was sure to crack a molar. Given that they were supposed to be in one of the warmest climes on the planet, she hadn't expected it to be this chilly at any point during this trip. But being on top of one of the world's tallest volcanos, it made sense if one thought about it. Especially at about four thirty in the morning. Well, that particular bit of wisdom wasn't doing her any good at the moment.

Their tour bus driver said they had to get here this early or all the viewing spots would completely fill up. If she'd known about the biting chill, she might have argued to take the risk. People around her were bundled up in coats and scarves. A few had thick, plush blankets. Even members of the wedding party had somehow come prepared. Had they received some kind of memo she hadn't?

Probably not, Rita thought and hugged her sweatshirt tighter around herself. They had just somehow planned better than she had. Story of her life. It wasn't even a terribly thick sweatshirt.

She heard a shuffling behind her and turned to find Clint approaching. She knew it was him, though it was somewhat hard to see in the pre-dawn darkness. He had a thick leather jacket on. Yet another person better prepared than she.

"You're shivering," he stated, noting the obvious.

"Ye-e-es. I—I a-a-am." Okay, so the stutter was a bit exaggerated. But not by much. Her lips were practically flapping together from the cold.

He started shrugging off his coat. "Here, take this."

She stopped him with a hand to his chest. "No way. I am not that s-selfish." The cold stutter made the word sound like she'd said *shellfish* and she had to stifle a laugh.

"I don't know you very well, but that's the last term I would use to describe you."

The words took her aback. In fact, she'd heard herself described that way countless times over the last several months. By people she cared for the most. When all she'd wanted to do was find her own way and discover what made her happy.

Correction, she'd wanted to discover what made her *feel*.

Though she didn't want to examine exactly what it was she was feeling right now. Neither did she want to admit that she'd been hoping Clint would find her at some point on top of this mountain.

"I can't take your coat," she insisted through the chattering.

"Well, I can't take watching you succumb to frostbite."

Before she knew what he was up to, he'd stepped behind her and enveloped her in his embrace, the coat wrapped around them both. "Here. In the interest of compromise."

A cocoon of heat suddenly surrounded her, along with his woodsy masculine scent. In her desire for warmth, she didn't bother to stop him or step away. Right. Like that was the only desire driving her at the moment.

"This is supposed to be one of the most spectacular sunrises on the earth. You don't want to turn into a frozen popsicle before you get to see it, do you?"

"I suppose not." She resisted the urge to snuggle her back closer to his chest. "Thank you."

He shrugged against her. "It's the least I can do. After the way you helped me the other night."

"Ah, you mean your evasion mission."

"It seems to have worked. Ms. Campbell seems to be wrapped around one of the other grooms-men at this very moment."

The way he was wrapped around her. "I'm sure she's simply trying to stay warm too."

"No doubt."

"She wasn't terribly happy with me that night after the luau when she came in," she told him, remembering the slamming of the suite door as she was brushing her teeth. Rita had felt some-what guilty. She had nothing against Tessa; they'd actually been study partners for some core sub-jects back in school. "I got a bit of the silent treat-ment before we both retired for the night."

"I think she may forgive you pretty soon. If she hasn't already. Judging by how she's moved on and all."

"I hope so. She did say one thing that night though."

She felt his warm breath against her cheek when he responded. "What's that?"

"She mentioned being surprised you were alone to begin with."

"So you guys were talking about me."

Uh-oh. "I won't deny it. Tessa said there had to be a story to explain why you were here stag at your own sister's wedding."

"Not really. Just one argument too many. Considering it wasn't a serious relationship, this seemed as good a time as any to end things. Rather than pretend during an island wedding full of activities. Some things simply aren't meant to be."

"I see. So it was mutual?" Rita wanted to bite her tongue as soon as the words left her mouth. She was giving Clint every indication that she was interested in his personal life. When she had absolutely no reason to be. No *logical* reason. She had to be careful. It would behoove her to be more guarded about such things, now that she was single again. "I'm sorry. It's not really any of my concern."

He remained silent at that. A strong gust of wind suddenly whipped through the air and she reflexively nestled closer against him.

Mistake.

A current of electricity shot through her core. She was no prude; she'd been a married woman for heaven's sake. But being in Clint's arms was triggering a reaction she hadn't been expecting. One she couldn't relate to anything else.

She'd loved Jay. She really had. But she couldn't recall feeling an electric jolt in the pit of her stomach when he held her. Not like she was feeling this very moment.

"What about you?" Clint surprised her by asking.

"Me?"

"If I recall, Lizzie mentioned a couple of years back attending a traditional Indian wedding. I believe you were the bride."

"You would be correct."

"But you're here alone."

"It's like you said, some things simply aren't meant to be."

He was silent for a moment, then she heard him take a deep breath. "I'm sorry."

"For?"

She felt his arms tighten around her. Sympathy? She certainly hoped not. "It's one thing when a short-term, frivolous relationship ends. A marriage failing is a bit more life altering."

He had no idea. The end of her marriage was only part of it. Someone like Clint would never understand. He could never grasp how someone like her had never truly felt untethered. She was a daughter first. Then a wife. Her identity had always been tied to someone else.

She'd never felt like just Rita. Just herself.

No, she wouldn't even bother to explain. There would be no point.

"Was it one particular thing?" he asked above her head. "That led to your split, I mean."

His question wasn't as simple as it appeared on the surface. There were so many particular smaller issues. And one major underlying one. "Yes. And no." It was the most honest answer she could give.

"So you're saying it's complicated."

She could repeat her answer and be correct once again. "Only in that we wanted different things." Things she was in no way ready for. While Jay wanted them more than anything. Things like a family, children, a house. Things she wouldn't be able to walk away from and then it would be too late, making her stay for all the wrong reasons. "So yes, in that way it was complicated."

She couldn't get into any more than that, despite Clint's charm and the effect he was having on her when he held her this way. How could she explain something that she hadn't fully grasped herself yet?

And what about him? What exactly was his story? The way he'd talked earlier about his relationships sounded as if he expected them all to come with predetermined expiration dates.

She was trying to come up with a way to ask when a small sliver of reddish-orange light broke through the surface of the clouds in the distance. The sun was finally beginning to rise. A collective hush suddenly fell over the murmuring crowd. In slow motion they all watched as more and more streaks of breathtaking hues of red broke over the sky.

The scene took her breath away. Any hint of her earlier cold or discomfort was completely forgotten. This view, this image would stay with her forever.

As would the thought that she was unexplainably happy that she'd been able to share it with Clint. While he held her in his arms.

The woman pulled at him like a magnet. Clint had fully intended to stay away from her on this trip. He really had. But then he'd seen her shivering in the dark with nothing but a flimsy, hooded sweatshirt and some type of thin fleece head-band. The windchill up here had to be below freezing at the least. How was he supposed to walk away?

He wasn't made of stone after all.

Now he was beyond happy that he'd ignored the warnings in his head and gone to her. He couldn't imagine taking in this scene any other way. Tomorrow he might think differently. But right now, watching the brilliant colors slowly explode across the dawn sky above the crater, he was more content than he could ever remember.

Spiritual. It was the one word that came to mind. The most spiritual thing he'd experienced in all his years. And he had the pleasure of doing so with the extraordinary woman who happened to be in his arms.

A few feet away, an elderly gentleman with long white hair dressed in traditional native garb began chanting.

"It's a prayer and salutation to the sun," Rita whispered below his ear. The chanter's deep, rich voice added yet another magical element to the extraordinary moment. Clint allowed himself to simply relax, to simply take in the majesty surrounding him. Rita was breathing steadily and deeply against his chest.

They remained that way several moments even after the sacred chant ended.

"That was amazing." Rita finally broke the silence but made no effort to move out of his embrace. And he couldn't remember when he'd ever felt so at peace, so serene.

The sound of someone clearing their throat behind them made them both jump. Clint turned to see his sister and her groom both staring with their mouths agape. Reluctantly, he pulled his arms away and let Rita go.

"I was really cold," Rita offered by way of explanation.

Lizzie blinked, then focused her intense gaze on her brother's face.

"She was shivering."

"Right" was Lizzie's only response but she dragged out the word so long it was almost comical. His soon-to-be brother-in-law made a dramatic gesture of coughing into his hand in order to hide his laugh.

Rita adjusted her top and stepped away. "That was quite an amazing sight to behold."

Clint had to tighten his fists to keep from

reaching for her again. As silly as that notion was under their current circumstances. But he couldn't deny that his fingers itched to do that very thing.

"Uh-huh. Sure was." Lizzie's double meaning was as clear as the new dawn sky behind them. He'd have to set the record straight with her at some point. Explain to her that he had no long-term sights on her school friend.

She really should know him better than that.

"So anyway," Jonathon finally said, "there's some hot chocolate and coffee waiting on the tour bus. The van with all the bikes is up here now. We'll be heading out shortly to ride." He tugged on his fiancée's hand. Lizzie finally moved and they both walked away.

Though Lizzie shot one more questioning look at him as they left.

"I'd almost forgotten," Rita said, not meeting his gaze. "About the biking."

Part of this excursion was to be a group bike ride back down the mountain. Apparently, it was the thing to do when you came up here.

"All part of the adventure."

Rita bit down on her lip and glanced up at the

road ahead. "I might have to skip that part of the experience."

That took him aback. "Whatever for? Can you ride?"

She nodded. "Yes, of course. But I've never actually ridden down a high, rugged mountain before."

He shrugged. "I'm guessing very few of us have."

She didn't respond.

"What will you do instead?" he asked her, suddenly beyond disappointed that she wouldn't be participating.

"I'll just ride down with the driver in the van."

He gave her a shrug. "I'm going to skip riding too then. I'll just drive down in the van with you."

"What? No. Why would you do that?"

"Well, I'm certainly not going to let you sit by yourself in the back of a van following the rest of us down as we ride. It's just not in my nature."

Her eyes clouded with concern. "I don't want to be the reason you miss out on this, Clint."

"Then reconsider. Come on, it will be fun."

Rita glanced at the road once more, apprehension clear in her expression.

"We'll go nice and slow."

She let out a deep sigh and rubbed her forehead. "All right. If you insist."

Clint couldn't help his smile of relief. He really hadn't been looking forward to the idea of being stuck in a van as everybody else got to enjoy the outdoor weather and mountainside sights. Not to mention, he figured he could use the physical exertion right about now.

Clint seemed to be exerting himself far more than the rest of them. Rita glanced behind her to check him once again. He was barely keeping up with the group. She was glad he'd talked her into going. She wasn't even sure why she had hesitated back there. Bike riding wasn't a new experience for her. And she'd always been pretty adventurous. Though something had changed within her since the divorce, something that made her second-guess her decisions as well as her abilities. She'd have to work on that.

Now there was no denying that the fresh air and the physical activity were serving to clear her head and invigorate her spirit.

But Clint seemed to be struggling behind her. Despite pedaling furiously and clearly straining, he seemed to consistently lag behind them all.

That made no sense whatsoever; the man was clearly fit. He appeared that way. Though, she'd have to admit, she'd seen more than her fair share of large muscular dogs like pit bulls and Dobermans who lacked stamina and energy.

Great. Now she was comparing the man to various breeds of canine.

Still, it was quite surprising. Especially considering they were going downhill and all. He didn't strike her as the type to fall behind when it came to anything. Let alone a physical activity. But hey, looks are deceiving. She knew that firsthand.

He'd certainly felt lean and muscular earlier this morning. Her mind darted back to the feeling of being held in his arms, snuggled against his chest. *Stop it.* Blinking the images away, she took the next turn perilously close to the edge. She didn't dare look over the side. They'd been given a full safety and precaution lecture, but nothing could have adequately prepared her for just how harrowing a ride this would be.

She really just needed to focus on her own ride and staying steady on the path.

A gurgle of laughter floated over to her from the front of the procession. She looked ahead to where Lizzie and Jonathon rode next to each other. They'd made some kind of game of trying to grab each other's hands, then letting go and quickly pedaling back to single file when the path became too narrow. How long the guide would let that continue was anybody's guess. But they seemed to be having a delightful time of it in the meantime.

Had she and Jay ever been that playful with each other? Had they ever shared such boisterous laughter? If so, she'd be hard-pressed to recall it.

That's what happened when you married out of a sense of loyalty rather than any kind of love or affection.

Clint had brought up her wedding. She hadn't thought about that day in ages. Though it had been a joyous occasion, she felt as though she'd sleepwalked throughout the entire ceremony and the events leading up to it. Her father had seemed so happy. Her mother the same simply by extension. A description that could pretty much summarize her parents' whole relationship.

Their families having been friends for years— since her father had immigrated—she and Jay had been thrust together pretty much their whole lives. He'd actually declared to her in third grade that he would take her as his wife. She'd stuck her tongue out at him.

And though her mom was as American as apple pie, Anna Paul had never questioned any of it. Again, another depiction that could define her mother's marriage to her father.

A grunt of noise behind her pulled her out of her thoughts. With a start, she realized it was Clint still straining to keep up. He'd broken out in a sheen of sweat. Was he ill?

A flash of concern shot through her chest. What if he wasn't feeling well? Maybe he was coming down with something. Luckily, the guide chose that moment to yell out that they'd be stopping for a water break at a rest area a few yards away.

Moments later, they had come to a complete stop.

"Are you okay?" she asked Clint when he finally pulled up next to her and disembarked from the bike.

"Must be the mountain air." He was as red as the sunset they'd just witnessed. "The brochure mentioned it might affect some people more than others."

"Maybe you should stop. Ask the guide to have the van come for you." No man she knew would go for that. They would take it as an insult to their very masculinity. But it was worth a try to make the suggestion.

"Maybe." To her surprise, Clint didn't immediately shoot down the idea.

Glancing over at his bike, Rita realized there was some kind of lever along the rails of his rear tire. One that wasn't there on hers. "Something's not right," she told him.

"What do you mean?"

"My back wheel looks different than yours."

He examined his bike, then studied hers. "You're right. Your bike's been running smooth?" he asked.

She nodded in reply. He bent and flipped some sort of gage on his back wheel. Something snapped in response on the bike's handlebars. Right then the guide came to stand next to them.

"Sorry, man. Mechanical malfunction. Looks like your brake was engaged this whole time."

Rita couldn't help it. Though she almost hated herself, she just couldn't help the bubble of laughter that erupted from deep within her chest.

"Oh, you think that's funny, do you?" Clint asked. But he wasn't trying to hide his own smile when he said it.

"I'm afraid so. I think it's hilarious."

Again surprising her, he threw his head back and laughed out loud himself.

Clint cursed out loud through his laughter. "Thank goodness you came along. Or I would have struggled with an engaged brake the whole time." He shook his head. "I can't believe it didn't occur to me to check that."

So the man could laugh at himself and didn't consider himself infallible. It was a novel experience for Rita to witness. She'd thought earlier about the lack of laughter between her and Jay. And here was yet another complete difference between the man before her now and the man she'd married. Jay would be taking the guide's name and information, making plans to call his superiors to complain about the oversight.

Enough. This wasn't some kind of schoolyard competition. She had to stop comparing this man she barely knew to her ex-husband.

Jay had been good to her. Even if some of his actions had felt patronizing and made her feel small, his heart had always been in the right place.

She really had no right to judge him so unfairly. Especially not after what she'd done to the man.

CHAPTER FOUR

TESSA WAS ALREADY in the shower when Rita got back to their room. And by the sound of things, she wasn't in there alone. Rita had to smile. Was there ever a time she herself had been that carefree? That determined to just go after what she wanted and just enjoy her life?

No, she never had. Maybe someday she'd reach that level of lightheartedness. Considering the way she'd grown up, it was going to take some time and some work.

As if on cue, her cell vibrated where she'd thrown it on the bed. A picture of her mother holding their shih tzu appeared on the small screen.

Opening the glass sliding door and stepping onto the balcony, she clicked on to answer the call. "Hey, Ma."

A family with three small children was playing some kind of tossing game in the yard right below their room. The gleam of the ocean shimmered in the distance. She tried to focus on those images rather than the expression that was sure to be on her mother's face an ocean away.

"Hello, dear. I finally got tired of waiting for you to call." Of course, the impetus was on her to be the first one to call. As always.

"Things have been very busy. Lizzie's packed a lot of activities into the schedule."

Rita could hear the notes of some bouncy hip-hop tune in the background. For as straitlaced and matronly as her mother was, she had some very eclectic tastes in music. Much to her father's chagrin. In so many ways, they were complete opposites. Maybe that was the secret of their success.

"How is dear Lizzie?" her mother asked. "Any wedding jitters?"

Rita thought about their playfulness during the bike ride. On the contrary, Lizzie and Jonathon seemed like they couldn't wait to tie the knot. "I haven't noticed any."

"Good. That's good to hear. I hope the two of them can make it work." The words *unlike you* hung unspoken in the air.

Rita bit back the response that popped into her head. Lizzie and Jonathon were so very different than she and Jay. For one, they'd actually chosen each other. "I think they will. All signs point in that direction."

"Good," her mom repeated. An awkward silence ensued in which all Rita could hear were some very racy lyrics about going to "da club." There was no way her father was home. Else he was on a completely different floor or puttering around in his garden outside.

"Jay came by the other day," her mother suddenly announced. "He asked about you."

A pang of sensation stirred within her chest. They had no business being married, but she missed Jay. She really did. One of the hardest things about the divorce was the fact that she'd felt like she lost a lifelong friend. Maybe over time they could become close that way once more. Another endeavor that was sure to take time, if it was possible at all.

"How is he doing?"

"He still seems quite morose, to be honest." A heavy pause followed which Rita figured she was supposed to fill. But what could she say to that? They'd gone over this before. The notion that perhaps Rita had been too hasty to end her marriage. Jay had pleaded with her to keep trying, claimed complete shock that she was ready to walk out. But she'd held firm. No reason to draw out the inevitable after all. Her husband showed no inclination to change. And she didn't know how.

Finally, her mother relented. After a long sigh, she continued, "His research is going well, at least. Said he was close to another patent. I get the impression he's thrown himself deeply into his work."

That made sense. There were times she hadn't seen him for days at a time. He'd disappear into the lab early and come home late. A slight wave of guilt hit her when she recalled how she'd mostly felt relieved those days, relishing the solitude and having the town house to herself. Jay had a very large personality. When he was around, there was no solitude to be found. "I'm glad he's doing well. On the professional front anyway. I know the rest will follow for him."

She heard her mother take a deep breath. "And what about you, love? Are you really doing well?"

She was. This trip away was exactly what she needed. Seeing Lizzie again, enjoying the majestic beauty of the island. Simply being in an environment so different from home, not to mention all the activities. She really hadn't anticipated enjoying a group bike ride down a rugged mountain. Clint had convinced her otherwise.

Clint. She couldn't deny she was enjoying his company. Perhaps more than she should have.

"Yes, Mom. I'm having a lot of fun here."

"Of course, you are, dear. But what about after?"

"After?"

"You're in paradise now, sweetie. What happens when you return and reality descends? I don't want you to regret your decisions. Now that it's too late to rectify any mistakes."

There was that word again. Some of the most important decisions she'd made in her life were ones her parents considered as her mistakes.

Rita rubbed her temple. Was it too much to ask just to live day by day? Did she always have to be focused on some future point off in the distance? "I'll be too busy to wallow, Ma. I have a lot to do when I get back."

For one, she'd have to look for another job. Perhaps she might finally find somewhere she could really make a difference. Although she loved the animals, she'd had her fill of the bureaucracy and constant focus on profit margins at her last position. She'd only taken the job to make Jay happy. Well, as happy as he was going to be when it came to her career.

"Your dad's threatening to retire. Again." Her mom suddenly changed the topic.

Speaking of people she missed. Though she'd seen her father plenty of times since the divorce, there seemed to be so much emotional distance between them now. Even more so than usual. "I'll believe it when I see it," she responded with a smile. Dad made that claim once or twice a year. Usually around wintertime, when he dreaded facing driving in the snow to his downtown office.

"He misses you." Rita sucked in a breath at her mother's words. The woman had always been very astute. And straightforward.

"I miss him too, Ma." She felt her eyes moisten with tears as she continued, "But I know I've disappointed him. Again."

"Oh, honey. He's your father."

"I think we'll just need some time. To find our way again with each other. I'm sure it will happen."

Sometimes, it was best just to tell her mother what she wanted to hear.

* * *

Clint watched from his balcony as a solitary figure made her way toward the water, strolling slowly, her head down. Even from this distance, there was no mistaking who it was. Rita. The slump of her shoulders and the drag in her step told him she wasn't exactly enjoying her slow walk along the beach. Something was on her mind.

It was none of his business really. This was one of the rare nights that Lizzie and Jonathon didn't have anything scheduled on an otherwise ridiculously packed itinerary. Good thing too. The excursion planned for tomorrow was a whole-day event: a ride down the Road to Hana, which apparently took several hours as a driver took them around the island and showed them many of the pertinent sights. So tomorrow would be completely spent.

And Clint had work to do. He'd already been away from his office for two straight days; there were a slew of emails waiting for him and several items that needed the CEO's signature.

The wise and prudent thing for him to do would be to pour himself a beer from the minibar, order some room service for dinner and fire up his laptop. But his eyes couldn't tear away from where Rita stood off in the distance. An unfamiliar tingle stirred in his chest. If he didn't know better, he'd think it was concern. Which made absolutely no sense. Aside from Lizzie, he'd never really been personally concerned about anyone's emotional state. Sure, he cared for his employees and made sure to take care of them, particularly the more loyal workers who had been with him from the beginning. It was those employees who deserved some of his attention right now in the form of email responses and returned phone calls. He was too hands-on not to be missed when away from the office.

Plus, as sweet as she was, he really had no business worrying about Rita Paul's mood.

He tore his gaze away from where she stood and turned back into the room. As soon as he booted up his computer, several messages scrolled across the scene. Clint rubbed his eyes. Yeah, it would be a long night of correspondence and directives. So he had to focus, which meant he had to keep his mind from drifting. Without meaning to, he looked up to glance toward the beach once more.

She'd moved. He could no longer see her. Had she gone back to her room? Walked farther along?

Damn. It didn't matter. He had work to do. Clint clicked on the first message and began to type.

She had to get used to this, Rita thought as she perused the menu she'd been handed. Being a single woman now, she had to get used to dining alone. What better time to start than a beachside seafood restaurant on exotic Maui?

At the table next to her sat a family of five with three young children. As frenzied as the parents looked, they posed a perfect picture of a happy unit. As the mom explained something on the menu to her preteen, her husband slowly rubbed a gentle hand down her back. True affection was clear in his absentminded movements. Rita forced herself to look away. Perhaps she'd have that someday. But that day was far-off.

As painful as it was, moments like this made her realize how right she'd been to end her marriage. She and Jay would never have been that couple sitting next to her right now. He may have loved her, but Jay wasn't the type to ever display affection in public. It seemed such a small thing, but small things sometimes made all the difference. She hadn't been able to explain that to him, or her parents for that matter, without feeling like she was being petty and childish. Rita thought back to the phone call earlier with her mother. Maybe they would never understand. Her ex-husband certainly didn't seem to still.

She found herself eavesdropping on the conversation at the next table. Having settled in with their appetizer as their children colored with fat, stubby crayons, the parents were now discussing the prospect of moving to a larger house. Rita watched as the man listened intently to his wife's thoughts and concerns on the matter. He reassured her they would make the correct decision when the time came. She responded with a small kiss to his cheek.

So different from any major discussion she'd ever had with Jay. In fact, when they were first engaged, her ex-husband had declared unequivocally that he had no intention of moving out of the condo he rented close to the university where he worked. It was understood that she would have to make herself at home at his place. She'd just accepted it. Then she'd been miserable. There'd been nothing overtly wrong with the place, but Rita had never felt like she truly belonged there.

Her attempts at redecorating had been met with resistance and resentment.

Jay liked his environment the way it was.

In retrospect, she had to admit that perhaps she should have held her ground, tried harder to exert her desires. But it hadn't seemed worth the effort. Her heart was never quite in it. Pulling her thoughts away from the past and from the conversation she had no business listening in on, she took a sip of her lemon water. No, her marriage had never been a true partnership, not like the one sitting at the next table anyway.

Was there a chance she would find that someday? Would she even have the gumption to risk her heart again? An unbidden image of chestnut-brown eyes and a dashing smile clouded her vision. Rita made herself blink it away and focus on her menu.

She honestly didn't know the answers. In the meantime, it looked like she'd be dining alone for a while.

He absolutely had to stay here and get some more of these emails answered. Clint stared at the screen until the words became a jumble of blurry swirls in his vision.

Focus.

He'd barely gone through a dozen or so messages. He had no business wondering about Rita and where she'd been heading. He absolutely could not go find her. It made no sense. And he was all about being logical and sensible.

So why did he suddenly stand and grab his shirt and sandals rather than clicking on the reply button of the message he'd been staring at for the past twenty minutes? Why was he out the door, making his way downstairs and outside before he could give it any more thought?

It didn't take long to spot her; she hadn't been moving very quickly after all. Clint watched as she went up to the maître d' podium of an outdoor restaurant, then was led away to one of the outer tables.

She sat down with a smile to the waitress, opened up her menu and seemingly ordered a drink. In a sea of tables, Rita sat by herself. When her drink arrived—some fruity concoction with an umbrella—she just stared at it for several moments. She was the only one eating solitary.

Damn.

This was silly. He couldn't very well just stand here staring at her any longer. How much time had passed anyway? Without allowing himself any further debate, he made his way to where she sat.

So deep in thought, she didn't seem to even hear him approach.

"A lei for your thoughts?" he said, clearly startling her out of her reverie.

"Clint." She gave him such a welcoming, radiant smile that it almost had his knees buckling with pleasure. Then she tucked a strand of hair that was blowing in her face behind her ear. It immediately escaped again from the wind. "I just thought I'd grab a bite."

"Are you waiting for someone?" he asked, though he was pretty sure he knew the answer.

She shook her head. "No, it's just me. What about you?" she asked. "How did you decide to come here?"

He didn't have it in him to lie. "I saw you out here and thought maybe you could use some company. You seem a bit...melancholy. If you don't mind my saying."

She didn't answer right away, instead turning to stare off into the distance. "You're a very observant gentleman, Clint Fallon."

And she was downright beautiful. The sinking

sun made her dark hair shimmer around her face; her lashes went on forever over piercing brown eyes. Clint had to suck in a breath and turn away to keep from staring at her.

"Have you eaten? I think I owe you a dinner," she suddenly proclaimed.

"Not yet. But I don't see why you would owe me anything."

"You saved me from certain frostbite early this morning. Remember?"

He'd been right about what he'd witnessed from the balcony. She was definitely nursing some kind of hurt. Her tone sounded down and defeated.

He'd never been accused of being the most attentive listener, but he could certainly lend an ear when he needed to, when the situation called for it. He heard a clear calling right now.

"I don't typically turn down pretty ladies who want to feed me." He pulled out the chair across the table from her and sat down.

A smile tugged at her mouth. "Does that happen to you often?"

"Not often enough."

"I find that hard to believe."

She motioned to the menu that sat in front of

him. "This place is supposed to be one of the best eateries in town. The concierge mentioned they have the best *hula* pies on the island."

"Moola pies? Sounds expensive."

Feeble a joke as it was, her smile grew wider. "*Hula* pies."

"What exactly is *hula* pie?"

"You'll have to experience it yourself."

"Thank you for the recommendation, ma'am. I look forward to it."

Sooner than he would have thought, the restaurant started to fill. They'd timed it right; the place was just on the verge of welcoming the evening dinner crowd and gradually becoming busier and busier.

In no time at all, almost every table was full and a line had formed outside the door all the way down to the beach.

"That was lucky. Timing it so that we don't have to wait for a table."

"If you're feeling lucky now, wait till you taste this pie." Her tone was whimsical but the merriment didn't quite reach her eyes.

What in the world could have brought her so down since their bike ride earlier today? He hoped she had grown comfortable enough with him to tell him whatever it was.

The waitress arrived to take their order. Clint ordered the *poke*, apparently some sushi dish that the menu said was the freshest this side of the sea, and a beer.

"I'll have the *hula* pie, please," Rita told her.

"Yes, miss. And for dinner?"

"I'm going with that as my dinner."

The waitress gave her an indulgent wink, then took their menus and left before returning with Clint's drink.

Clint chuckled. "Ice cream, chocolate, coconut and nuts. I suppose that covers most of the food groups."

"Sometimes a girl's just looking to have dessert."

"One of those afternoons?"

"You could say that."

"Please don't tell me my sister's pulling some bridezilla moves and hassling her bridesmaids."

She shook her head. "No, nothing like that. I haven't even seen Lizzie since this morning's bike ride."

"Phew, I didn't want to have to reprimand her at her own wedding."

She gave him a curious look at that statement, then reached for her cocktail. He tried not to focus too closely on her lips when she lifted the cherry and popped it in her mouth. "Just a phone call from back home. I let it affect me more than I should have."

"Must have been one heck of a phone call. You just ordered dessert for dinner. Not that there's anything wrong with that."

"There are people who might not agree with you on that point. They'd see plenty wrong with it."

The ex. She had to be talking about him. Perhaps that had been who her misbegotten call had been with. He clenched his fists on the table and had to take a swig of his beer. The idea that she stayed in touch still with her former husband left a bad taste in his mouth. But again, none of his business.

"Anyone in particular we're talking about?"

She took another sip of her drink, looked out over the horizon at the setting sun. Though the scene held no comparison to the breathtaking visual of the sunrise they'd watched this morning, the sheer magnitude of vibrant color in the Hawaiian sky was a sight to behold.

"Could easily apply to several people actually. People who are very focused on rules and structure and propriety."

Oh, yeah. She definitely had something on her mind. "Nothing wrong with rules and structure," he told her. "As long as those rules serve a purpose and make sense."

"I suppose you're right."

"I think so. I wouldn't be able to run an international construction firm if I didn't adhere to some type of structure and follow it rigidly."

"Run a tight ship, do you?" She asked with a hint of a smile.

No doubt about it. Not when his reputation and livelihood were on the line. The slightest mistake could cost big. Both in terms of dollars and time. Not to mention, the risk to lives if proper safety protocols weren't followed. When it came to his company, Clint kept as much as feasible under his tight control. Down to the specific types of screws and nails to be used at all of his sites. "I have to run a tight ship. A lot can go wrong on a construction site. Especially when you're talking tall buildings. Can't leave anything to chance."

She chuckled at that and started fidgeting with her napkin. "You sound very much like some-

one else I know. That's a favorite phrase of his."
Raising her glass in a mock salute, she cleared
her throat. "You can't leave anything to chance."
Her tone was exaggeratingly deep.

"Sounds like a wise man. Want to tell me who
you might be referring to?" Though he could
guess. It didn't take a mind reading ability to
figure who she meant.

"I will tell you. Probably because I've had half
of this very strong drink on an empty stomach."

He doubted the fruity cocktail—complete with
a paper umbrella—could be that potent. She was
clearly a lightweight. "Maybe you should slow
down."

"I'm talking about my ex," she said, ignoring
his warning. "More than once, he tried to teach
me a lesson about why I should be more disci-
plined and not leave things to chance."

Taught her a lesson? The hair on the back
of Clint's neck stood up as a bolt of fury shot
through him. His vision blurred. If that pitiful
excuse for a man had so much as harmed a hair
on her, he'd make it a life goal to find him and
do some score settling.

"Rita. Did he hurt you in any way?" he asked
steadily through tightly clenched teeth.

She blinked. "What? No. That's not what I mean," she said with a dismissive wave of her hand.

Clint let out the breath that had caught in his throat. "Then what do you mean exactly? About teaching you a lesson?"

"Exactly that. Jay's a medical researcher at a prominent university. He's used to controlling every variable. I'm a bit more carefree. He simply took some pains to show me why his way was right and mine was foolish."

"I don't follow."

She leaned forward on the table, steepled her fingers. "There was the time we were grocery shopping. I walked away down another aisle. I left my purse in the cart. I knew exactly what I was going to get and where it was." She glanced off to the side, as if recalling the exact memory. "When I got back to the cart moments later, my purse was gone."

He was starting to see where this might be going. "Let me guess, he'd warned you repeatedly not to leave your bag unattended."

She raised her glass. "A toast to you for the right answer. I got a scathing lecture about how right he'd been. How reckless and senseless it was of me to walk away from the cart that held my wallet, my keys, my money."

All right. It sounded like it might have been harsh for her to hear. But many husbands would have reacted the same way.

But Rita's hands were trembling as she recalled the story.

"I was panicked," she continued. "My phone, my license. Everything was in that bag."

"I guess he could have been a bit more understanding." Still, it hardly seemed like an unforgivable reaction. She had been rather careless to leave the purse unattended.

She laughed but it sounded less than jovial. "There's a surprise ending to this story."

"What's that?"

Her fingers tightened on the stem of her glass. "He's the one who'd taken it. He'd walked all the way back to the parking lot and to our car and thrown it in the trunk."

That *was* a surprise ending. Clint had definitely not seen that twist coming. Words failed him. Who would do something like that?

"What happened?" he finally managed to utter.

"After several minutes of panicked searching, during which he coldly stood by and watched by the way, I finally asked for his phone so I could notify the authorities about the theft of my personal belongings. That's when he finally told me he'd had it the whole time."

Clint downed the rest of his beer. He couldn't imagine doing such a thing to another person, especially someone he supposedly loved. It seemed so… *Petty* was the one word that came to mind.

"That was just one example," Rita added, polishing off her drink, as well.

"There was more?"

She nodded. "Little things. He insisted on being in charge of my online passwords because I didn't change them often enough. He kept asking how I planned to be a responsible mother one day if I couldn't keep track of little details such as security codes. So, ultimately, I decided that I wasn't even ready to be a wife. Let alone a mother."

Clint needed another drink. But the waitress was nowhere to be found. To think, this accomplished, intelligent, talented woman before him was thought to be careless and in need of strict guidance by the man she'd married.

"I had to walk away. The controlling became too much," she said on a sigh.

He couldn't help himself. He reached across the table and took her hand in his. "I'd say that behavior sounds a bit beyond controlling." Much more. In fact, the word *belittling* came to mind.

CHAPTER FIVE

HER HEAD POUNDED like a slow hammer when she awoke the next morning. There was a reason she generally tried to stay away from hard liquor. If she'd only stuck with her usual cabernet, she wouldn't be feeling so foolish this morning.

Though she couldn't bring herself to regret a single moment of it. Sitting there with Clint in that restaurant, she could almost pretend she was a regular young adult on an exciting date with a new man. Not a recent divorcée who was just sharing a meal with her friend's brother. Her friend's handsome, charming and beyond alluring brother.

A smile touched her lips when she thought of the joy that had flooded her chest when she'd looked up to find he'd followed her, that she wouldn't have to eat alone after all. A silly girlish giggle escaped her lips before she bit down on it. How foolish of her.

In any case, she should have definitely gone

easier on the mixed drinks. But no, she'd had to indulge. And look where it had gotten her. She'd ended up letting her tongue loose and way over-sharing with Clint Fallon. A man she had nothing in common with. A man she would probably never see again after this wedding was over.

And in the meantime, she had to spend a whole day with him and the rest of the wedding party in a large van as they traveled the Road to Hana.

He'd caught her at a vulnerable time, she thought as she summoned the elevator—this time unable to face the stairs—to take her down to the front entrance where the shuttle would be picking everyone up. Phone calls from her mother tended to put her in such a state. She'd simply meant to take a walk along the beach to shake off the doldrums of her conversation, then check out the restaurant she'd heard so much about since arriving.

But then he'd shown up.

Rita stepped into the glass elevator and watched the scenery outside as the unit began to descend to the first-floor lobby. There was no denying her immediate reaction upon seeing him last night though. There was no denying her reaction to him in general.

The truth was, a wave of pleasure had bloomed in her chest when she'd seen him arrive to eat with her last night. Electricity had crackled between them all during dinner, even after she'd overconfided.

And how foolish was that? They were from two different worlds. He'd accomplished so much and her life was in complete shambles. Before she could even think about any kind of attempt at a relationship, she had to repair everything that had gone so wrong these past couple of years.

Starting with repairing the relationship with her father.

The only sound thing to do today would be to avoid Clint Fallon altogether. She would appreciate the sights, take lots of photos, talk to everybody else and try to enjoy herself. With a sigh of relief about her decision, she stepped outside through the sliding doors of the front hotel entrance.

The bus was almost completely full by the time she got on. She passed Lizzie and Jonathon in the front row. They were too engrossed with each other to take any notice of her. Seat after seat was taken.

The only one she didn't see yet was Clint. Rita

continued slowly making her way to the back of
the bus. Tessa smiled at her from one of the middle seats, next to a groomsman Rita didn't know
by name. Probably the shower buddy from the
other night. Still no Clint. There was definitely
a pattern. Every seat held a man/woman pairing. Looked like there was a lot of hooking up
going on.

Oh, great, she could see where this was headed.

There were times Rita was sure the universe
was simply laughing at her. This was clearly one
of those times.

She found Clint in the final row. With the only
open spot left on the bus next to him. He scooted
over and gestured for her to sit. Like she had a
choice. "Looks like everyone has paired up," he
said as he scooted over. "Kind of leaves you and
I as odd men out."

Which essentially had the effect of pairing
them up as well, Rita thought, trying not to groan
out loud.

So much for the Fallon-avoidance plan.

Within an hour, they'd reached their first stop.
Somehow, the day had grown cloudy with a slight
mist of rain. The change in weather did nothing to diminish the sight however. They were on

top of a lookout that showcased several majestic waterfalls.

The pairing on the bus didn't disperse as everyone exited the vehicle. Several of the couples held hands. More than a few relationships had apparently formed over the short time they'd been in Hawaii.

She walked over to one of the railings and leaned on the metal, simply taking in the view. Sure enough, Clint appeared beside her within moments. He leaned over the banister, as well.

"If you want some alone time, just let me know."

She couldn't even be sure if that's what she wanted. Her emotions and feelings were just a mishmash of confusion right now.

"But it seems a shame not to share the beauty of this experience with someone else," Clint added.

He was right, of course. This was silly. They were both adults. They might even be considered friends.

She gave him a slight smile, not turning away from the view. "I thought maybe you'd be tired of my rambling. I did somewhat talk your ear off last night."

"Do you really believe that?"

No, she didn't. Clint was genuine and attentive. He'd listened to her and sympathized last night. Not once had she felt a hint of judgment on his part. Exactly what someone would want if they were looking for a confidant.

She hadn't realized how much she needed that, just to have someone listen. Without any criticism, unlike her parents whenever the matter came up. Her girlfriends were all too quick to try to reassure her that the divorce was for the best, just like Lizzie had the day of arrival. Hard to believe Clint Fallon was the first person to give her a chance to finally get some of the turmoil off her chest. It was more than just the drink. She'd found Clint surprisingly easy to talk to, to confide in.

Still, thinking back on the exchange now, she felt raw and exposed. "I didn't mean to share that much," she admitted.

He waited a while before answering. "I'm really glad you did."

Clint resisted the urge to gently nudge Rita's head onto his shoulder. She'd fallen asleep as they drove to their next stop on the tour. She didn't look terribly comfortable with her head bent at an odd angle against the seat. He wasn't sure how she'd react, given how regretful she seemed about their time together last night at dinner. She couldn't think he thought any less of her because of what she'd told him about her failed marriage. If anything, he'd been struck by her strength and resilience in the face of such a situation. Someone should have really told her that at some point.

He was spared further internal debate about moving her when they finally reached their next destination: one of the Seven Sacred Pools of 'Ohe'o. He gave Rita a soft tap on the shoulder to wake her up. She opened her eyes with a start.

"Sorry. But we're here. I didn't think you'd want to sleep through the Seven Sacred Pools visit."

Rubbing her eyes, she stood and stretched out her legs. The innocent gesture sent a bolt of awareness through him. He gave himself a mental snap. Resilient or not, the woman was reeling from a broken relationship. He had no business staring at and appreciating her legs. Shapely and alluring as they may be.

"Thanks. Guess I was more tired than I realized. Did I miss anything along the ride?"

Clint shook his head, then stood to join her in the aisle of the van. "Only an interesting dissertation about lava tunnels from our expert tour guide/driver. He seems to know quite a bit. Both about the geography and folklore. Said he was born and raised on Maui." Okay, he was clearly rambling. But they'd already had a few moments of awkwardness between them so far this morning. He found himself missing the easy camaraderie of the previous evening. It couldn't have been totally alcohol driven, could it?

"You'll have to fill me in on the rest at some point," she said as they exited the van.

This was one of the spots they'd been told to pack bathing suits for. A lush green mountainside with several small waterfalls surrounded a pool of crystal-blue water. It was apparently one of the most popular spots for tourists to take a dip in. A few of the visitors already there were jumping into the water off some of the lower cliffs.

"This is one of the seven legendary pools," their tour guide and driver said to their quickly dispersing crowd, raising his voice to be heard. "It is said that a dip in these pools will lead to good fortune and the finding of true love." He scanned the wedding party. Several couples were already in the water, giggling and splashing around. Tessa had jumped onto her groomsman's back as he playfully ducked under the water to get her wet. Jonathon had his arms wrapped around Lizzie's waist as they waded into the pool.

"Then again, it looks like you all might not need it," the tour guide added with a light chuckle.

A heady idea suddenly occurred to Clint. He turned to Rita standing next to him. "Would you like to come with me?"

She gave him a questioning look. "To swim?"

"Sort of. I think we should try jumping off a cliff."

Rita was determined to make the best of the way this day was turning out. Clearly, she and Clint were the only people in the wedding party who hadn't hooked up, so to speak. Well, good for them. As for her, she was going to make the most of this adventure, enjoy the company of the man saddled with her for now and try to just enjoy herself in general.

Though she hadn't exactly planned to start with a jump into a deep pool of water off a rocky cliff. Some of which didn't seem terribly high, but still.

"Are you with me?" he asked her. "You can swim, right?"

"It's not the swimming part that I'm grappling with."

"Come on. It'll be fun. I'll lead the way and stay with you the whole time." With that, he took her hand and they started making their way along the slippery, wet rocks surrounding the edge of the water. She'd never seen such greenery, such lush plant life. She'd never cliff jumped before.

But despite her apprehension, she'd be a fool to miss out on any of this. If just for today, she was going to forget about the shambles her life had become, forget about the depressing phone call with her mother yesterday and try to fully immerse herself in this adventure.

To his credit, Clint kept to his word and steadied her the whole way up. If he would do a cliff jump with her, he'd probably follow her anywhere. Pretty soon, they found themselves perched on the precipice of a jutting boulder along the side of the mountain about ten feet above the water.

"Is this a good spot?" Clint asked.

"Well, I'm not going up any farther, if that's what you mean." Though now she was looking down, she wasn't quite sure even this was too high.

Clint chuckled. "We can jump in together, if you'd like," he said, taking her hand once more. Her fingers reflexively curled around his. She'd been trying not to look at him too closely after he'd taken his shirt off earlier. The man was fit. A solid chest, taught, defined muscles, skin already a deep rich tan.

"Are you having second thoughts about this?"

More like I'm having unwanted thoughts about you.

She shook her head. "I think maybe we should just jump before I start to though."

"You're sure you're comfortable in the water?"

"Oh, yes." The water part wasn't the issue. It was the whole launching herself off a cliff thing. How in the world had she allowed herself to get talked into this? Why did she get the impression she wouldn't even be attempting it if Clint wasn't by her side? And what exactly did that mean for her mental state when it came to him?

This was so not the time to contemplate it.

"In that case—" He didn't finish, just tugged her along with him as they both jumped off.

Rita felt herself hit the water with a resounding splash. Exhilaration pumped through her veins as she broke the surface, laughter erupting in her throat.

Clint still held on to her hand.

"That was amazing."

"Hope I didn't take you by surprise, tugging you in like that."

"Oh, but you did." She playfully splashed him. "And you don't regret it at all, do you?"

He laughed in return. "Figured you didn't need too much time to think about it."

She dived under the surface, allowing the coolness of the water to refresh her both in body and spirit. If she had to work hard to have fun and forget her troubles for a while, then so be it. Though she had to admit, having Clint around was making the endeavor easier than it otherwise would have been. Too easy.

All too soon, the guide signaled that their party should probably start toweling off and return to the van. Reluctantly, Rita followed as Clint guided her toward the edge of the pool and helped her out. Their guide handed them thick towels.

"Thanks for doing that with me." Clint rubbed the towel around his head to dry off his hair. The strands were a mess of spikes around his head when he was done. Somehow the look did nothing to diminish the rugged handsomeness of his face. The wetness turned his locks from a dark brown to jet-black that brought out the golden specks in his eyes.

Rita looked away and focused on getting herself dry. But she couldn't hide the shiver than ran over her skin, only partially due to the chill of being wet. The sun had poked through a thick cloud while they'd been swimming but it was still somewhat overcast.

"Here." Clint stepped over to her and draped his towel over her shoulders.

"Thanks—you keep helping me to stay warm, it seems." Not to mention, the exciting things he'd been convincing her to try. As if something happened to her cautious inhibitions around this man.

The clap of the guide to summon them cut off Clint's response. He followed her to the van and they both got on board.

"You may be wondering why these pools are full of fresh water when they touch the sea," the guide began, using a microphone to address his many passengers. Part of the experience of the tour was a continuing commentary about the island and the sites they were visiting. Rita found it charming. The driver was personable and well-spoken, a good fit for the job he was in. "There are many theories, some more scientific than others."

"We want to hear one of the nonscientific theories," Lizzie declared from the front and Rita saw Jonathon give her shoulders an indulgent squeeze. A collective shout of agreement chorused from the others.

"Anything for the customer," the guide said into his mic. "There's a particularly sad legend about a princess and her lost love."

Rita settled back into her seat; Clint's warmth next to her and the deep voice of the driver lulled her into a meditative state of relaxation that she more than welcomed.

The man proceeded to tell a wrenching story that had to be based on at least some truth—that thought made her heart ache—about a princess who fell deeply in love with one of her guards. But she was honor and duty bound to marry a prince from another neighboring native tribe, one her father had picked for her.

The princess turned her back on her true love in order to perform her expected duties and married a man she didn't care for. He turned out to be cruel and vicious. In a fit of rage and jealousy, he killed the princess when he thought she was being unfaithful. He had incorrectly mistaken one of her handmaidens for another man as both male and female islanders wore their hair long past their hips. Finding out about his error made him irrationally even angrier.

So just for good measure, he searched out the man who had first claimed the princess's heart and brutally murdered him, as well.

"So every night, the ghost of the poor princess sheds enough fresh tears into the pools to flood out all the salt water." With that, the guide rehung his mic into its slot on the dashboard.

A quietness settled over the cabin of the van. The overall mood had definitely turned to the somber side.

Rita knew it was simply a story, most likely based on generations of native folklore. But the lesson and theme was a universal one and she found herself instinctively nestling closer to the man sitting next to her.

"Next stop is Black Sand Beach." The driver's voice crackled through the vehicle's intercom system and pulled Rita out of her thoughts. She'd been thinking about the sorrowful story of the princess since they'd left the last location.

"Ready for the next adventure?" Clint asked as they pulled to a stop. Another breathtaking scene of visual magic greeted them when they disembarked.

A wide pathway led to a steep stairway that took them down to a beach unlike any she'd seen before.

The sand, the pebbles, the boulders that met the crashing waves were all completely black. As if some divine hand had taken a tub of ebony paint and brushed wide strokes over the entire area.

"Amazing, isn't it?" Clint asked her.

"I don't have the words." She turned to him. "Thank you for this. Really. I would have never seen any of this if it hadn't been for you. And Lizzie."

He ducked his head like a small boy almost. She'd embarrassed him. "More so Lizzie. She and Jonathon coordinated with a planner and booked every tour and excursion."

He wasn't going to take any of the credit, even if he was bankrolling the whole thing. As far as big brothers went, Lizzie had hit the jackpot.

"There's a cave over there." Clint changed the

subject before she could say any more about his part in all the wonder they were experiencing. "I say we go explore."

Without waiting for an answer. He pulled her behind him and led her into the mouth of a cavern. Not that she would have said no in any case.

It was like stepping into another dimension. All the noises outside went suddenly mute. Other than the opening, the area around them was pitch-black. The walls shimmered with moisture. A sudden cold wetness ran over her sandaled feet. The unexpected sensation jolted her; she lost her balance and startled to topple backward.

A set of steel-hard arms immediately wrapped around her waist and pulled her upright. She found herself hauled against a hard, broad chest.

"We've got to stop meeting like this," Clint said hoarsely against her ear. The heat of his breath sent a tingle along her skin. It would be so easy to turn to him, to totally succumb to the warmth and security of his embrace.

"You seem to keep rescuing me. Starting at the airport."

She felt him chuckle more than she heard it. "You're hardly the type of woman who needs rescuing, Rita."

Did he really mean that? Did he see her that way? As someone strong? Independent?

She felt heady at the thought. So many times in her life, the people she loved the most made sure to point out all the ways she was *less*. So often, Rita had spent all her energy trying to simply prove them wrong. But this man before her now seemed to think otherwise, he seemed to see her as *more*. It was a new experience.

A peal of laughter from outside the cave spiked through the air and pulled her back to reality.

"We should go with the others," she said.

Clint hesitated a beat but slowly let her go. "Yeah, you're right."

Rita sucked in a breath of air as she followed and gave herself a mental shake. She had to keep her bearings about her. The exotic location and all the excitement was making her act with uncharacteristic recklessness. For one insane moment, she'd thought about kissing him. Her fingers went to her lips as she wondered what that might have felt like, what he might have tasted like.

No. She had to accept that this was part of some dreamlike fantasy that she was unlikely to encounter again. Reality would return soon enough and she had to be ready for it.

But she would never forget the things he'd said to her, the way he'd made her feel for the brief moment when it was just the two of them in this empty cave. She reached down and picked up one of the small black rocks from the ground. Turning it in the palm of her hand, she slipped it into the pocket of her jean shorts.

No, she would never forget standing in a tight, dark cave with Clint nor the feelings the close proximity elicited within her. But she wanted a memento nevertheless.

CHAPTER SIX

CLINT DESPERATELY WANTED a shower. Preferably a cold one. The colder the better. Then he was going to find an aged bottle of fine bourbon and spend the night on his balcony drinking and willing away the thoughts that were sure to plague him after the day he'd just spent.

With Rita.

He would have to try hard not to think about all the times her leg had brushed along his in the seat during the drive. All the times the car had gone around a curve and her delicious, supple body had slid up against him.

And he absolutely could not think about the way she'd felt in his arms after they'd jumped into the sacred pool together. She'd almost said no to that. Just as she'd originally balked at the bike ride. Rita must have taken quite a hit to her confidence these past few months. She just needed a nudge to show her how capable and competent she was. A small hint of pride sparked in his chest that he'd been the one she'd allowed in enough to do so.

He'd wanted so badly to kiss her in that secluded cave. He could imagine even now how she would taste.

It was going to be a hell of a night.

Right now, they were all spilling into the lobby after several hours spent seeing the sights and attractions along the Road to Hana. It had been a long day. Fun but tiring. The kind of day that would normally end for him with a cold drink in his hand and a warm body in his bed. An unbidden image of dark chocolate eyes and silky black hair popped into his mind before he pushed it away.

He'd had way too much fun with Rita. Every stop made more enjoyable with her accompanying him. So much so that he didn't want it to end. But it would have to. If she was anyone else, he'd ask her to join him on that balcony. To share that drink with him and let the rest of the evening take its natural course.

But no. Not this time. Not with this woman.

He didn't do long-term relationships and she wasn't the kind to have a fling with. Especially considering she was still licking her wounds after a recent divorce.

Oh, and there was also that whole thing about her being a close friend of his younger sister's. There were all sorts of ways a careless move with Rita could get messy and complicated.

Logic dictated that he simply bid her good-night and hope he'd see her again tomorrow morning. He turned to do just that but was abruptly cut off by Lizzie's angry shriek from across the lobby.

"How could you say something like that?" she demanded of her fiancé, her cheeks blazing red with fury. "You can be such an ass sometimes."

"What did you just call me?" For his part, Jonathon looked equally as enraged.

"You heard me."

Clint debated going over there to pull one or the other to the side. They'd started to attract the attention of other guests. The night manager behind the desk looked as if he was trying to decide the same thing. The man had gone pale and swallowed hard.

"I would hate to have to burden you with an ass for a husband," Jonathon fired back.

Lizzie's eyes narrowed on Jonathon's face.

"What's that supposed to mean? What exactly is it that you're trying to say?"

Clint uttered a curse under his breath. He really wished she hadn't asked him that. Jonathon's reply was exactly what he'd feared it might be.

This did not bode well.

"Maybe this is a mistake, Lizzie," Jonathon bit out through clenched teeth. "Maybe we should call off the whole thing."

Lizzie's gasp of horror was audible; she visibly bit back a sob. Clint started forward but felt a small hand grab him about the wrist. He turned to see Rita shaking her head slowly at him, a clear warning in her eyes.

His sister brushed past him as she fled the lobby. Jonathon stomped off in the opposite direction, leaving everyone else in the lobby staring agape.

Several bridesmaids and groomsmen turned to him, as if awaiting some sort of explanation. Like he had any idea what had set the whole argument off. Last he'd seen, the two had been all over each other on the bus.

"Show's over, folks," he said to the collective crowd. Several moments passed but eventually, one by one, everyone started to disperse.

All except for Rita.

She cleared her throat next to him. "I hope you understand why I stopped you from going to them."

He sighed. "Yes. You were right. Nothing would have been gained by me getting in the middle of that." He turned to look her straight in the eye. "I owe you a thank-you for averting it." He could have very well made things much worse. Though it looked bad enough already.

"They probably both just need some time," Rita said. "Weddings can be really stressful. Once they've had a chance to cool off, I'm sure they'll both be ready to make up."

He certainly hoped so. Otherwise, he'd have a huge mess on his hands. All the pending arrivals would need to be notified. Contracts would need to be canceled. There was no way he'd see any kind of refund for anything. Not at this late stage.

Not that any of that mattered. Lizzie would be miserable and that tugged at his heart. She deserved to be happy.

The manager appeared by them, his cheeks a slight pink. "Any way I may be of service, Mr. Fallon?"

"Yes, please. Send a bottle of your house merlot and some snacks to my sister's room. Please add a card that says she knows where to find me if she needs."

"Right away, sir."

Clint turned to see Rita eyeing him, a curious glint in her expression. "What?" he asked.

She shook her head. A soft smile graced her lips. "I think you could use a drink yourself. Can I interest you in joining me for one?"

All his earlier intentions of avoidance fled in that very instant. Nothing in the world could have possessed him to turn her down in that moment, not when she was looking at him like that.

"I'd be very interested," he told her, ignoring the cry of warning in his head.

The moon cast silver light on the sand next to their table at the outdoor bar of the resort. Foamy waves crashed against land a few feet away from where they sat. Rita ran her finger around the rim of her wineglass. She didn't really want the drink, felt tired down to her bones after the day they'd just had.

There was no denying that Lizzie and Jonathon's argument had shaken her. They'd seemed so happy together just a few short hours ago. The thought of the two of them breaking up just before their wedding was almost too much to bear. There was no way she would be able to fall asleep with all that on her mind.

Plus, she had to admit she didn't want to say goodbye to Clint just yet. There was nothing scheduled for tomorrow. No excursions, no meals with the wedding party.

She realized she dreaded the idea that the whole day might go by without seeing him. That thought sent a surge of guilt through her chest. She should be worrying about her friend and the possibility her engagement may have ended just days before she was due to be married. Instead, here Rita sat, overly concerned about spending time with that friend's brother.

What was it about this particular man that called to her so strongly? Her friends had warned about being on the rebound and falling too quickly for someone. But this didn't feel like a rebound scenario. Not that she could really know for sure. All of this was so new to her.

She hadn't really dated anyone seriously. And as soon as she was old enough, her father had subtly pushed her toward Jay in so many nuanced and not-so-nuanced ways.

If ever there was someone who should tread carefully when it came to the opposite sex, she would be the poster child.

"I wonder what triggered that whole thing," Clint said after taking a small sip from his drink. The thick amber liquid in his glass told her it was something strong which would probably make a lightweight like her gag if she tried it.

"Lizzie and Jonathon's argument, you mean?"

He nodded. "I'm guessing it was something she was being stubborn about. She can be a little self-centered." He sighed and looked out toward ocean. In the distance the water looked as black as the cave they'd been in earlier. The cave where she'd fallen into Clint's strong arms when he'd caught her before she could fall.

Don't go there.

"I blame myself for that," he added. "For how stubborn and self-centered my little sister can be."

"I think you're giving yourself too much credit. Or fault, in this case."

He shrugged. "Maybe. But I was the one responsible for her."

"You're not that much older than her, Clint."

"That may be so. But after our parents died, there was no one else."

Rita knew a bit about their struggles as teens after the passing of their mom and dad. They'd been sent to live with a maternal grandmother who was way past the age of being able to care for two grieving and active teenagers. Lizzie hadn't really talked about it much at school, but there'd been enough times when she'd opened up.

From what Rita understood, Clint had started working as soon as he was of age to help care for himself and his sister. By the time Rita had met her, Lizzie's brother was already on his way to becoming a multimillionaire tycoon with his own construction firm with satellites all over the nation.

Quite extraordinary if one thought about it.

"Oh, Clint," she began, unable to keep the sudden emotion out of her voice. "You had to grow up pretty fast, didn't you?"

He looked off into the distance toward the water. "Not by choice."

He was so wrong about that. "You did have a choice. You could have left Lizzie to her own devices. Or tried to get your grandmother to step up."

He laughed at the idea. "Yeah. That wasn't

going to happen. It was clear within months of us moving in with her."

"What do you mean?"

"Nothing specific. Just that money was always tight. My parents didn't exactly save for a rainy day. Too busy spending it all on their travels and adventures. What little they left, my grandmother put away. Never let us touch it. We were in a new school, the kids ready to pounce at our clear disadvantages. The girls were particularly hard on Lizzie. For having to wear the same clothing and shoes to school almost every day."

"What did you do?"

He rubbed a hand down his face. "It's not important."

She leaned closer across the table. "Please tell me."

He hesitated so long, Rita thought he might not answer. Finally, he let out a deep sigh. "What could I do? I got several odd jobs so that we could have some kind of spending money. It wasn't much, just tips from busing tables at a restaurant and lawn mowing money. But it was something."

She thought of the boy he must have been, the sheer effort and discipline it must have taken for him to rise to where he was.

An urge to go to him, wrap her arms around his shoulders to comfort and soothe him almost overwhelmed her. She fought it. Hard.

"Thanks again for making sure I didn't get in the middle of their argument," he told her. "I wasn't even sure what I would have said. Or which one of them I would have said it to."

"It never works out well when a third party tries to intervene in a relationship."

Clint didn't say anything for several beats, just studied her face. "You sound like you're speaking from experience."

She allowed herself a laugh that held no real humor. "I suppose I am. To this day, both my parents seem to think I was the one who managed to ruin a good marriage. My mom is a bit more vocal about it but my father's feelings have been made clear, as well. Many times."

He reached for her hand across the table and held it tightly in his. The warmth of his skin sent a tingling sensation up her arm and straight to her heart. "I'm sorry you had to deal with that, Rita. You deserve so much more."

"Thank you for that." She ducked her head. "I wouldn't want either Lizzie or Jonathon to feel that way. Not even for a moment."

He gave her hand another squeeze before slowly letting it go.

"I just hope they figure it out soon." He let out a small chuckle and rubbed a hand down his face. "Who knows. Maybe this is happening because someone didn't pay heed to the curse our tour guide warned us about."

"Curse? I didn't hear anything about a curse." Just that terribly sad story about the heartbroken princess who'd tried to do right by her family and tribe only to be murdered.

Clint polished off his drink. "You might have been sleeping. He said nothing should be removed from any of the beaches we visited. Not even so much as a pebble. Or it would lead to doom and bad luck."

Rita felt a slow sinking in her chest. She'd taken that small rock. But surely it was just a silly superstitious story. She'd simply wanted a small souvenir.

Her small transgression could absolutely *not* be the reason the bride and groom were fighting at this very moment. And threatening to call off the wedding.

"It sounds like mere superstition," Rita said,

voicing her thoughts, just as their waitress appeared. "Island folklore."

Their server smiled at them. "What folk story are you referring to?" The young lady asked with a friendly smile. Her name tag said Tanna in curly black lettering. "I come from several generations of native Hawaiians. I may know it."

"The superstition that says removing anything from Black Sand Beach will result in misfortune."

Tanna shook her head vehemently. "Oh, no. That one's real. Those beaches are sacred. Nothing is to be removed. It's absolutely bad luck."

Rita felt her stomach drop. This was just silly. She hadn't even known she was doing anything wrong!

Tanna continued, "It is very easy to anger the spirits. Every pebble, every rock, every grain of sand is exactly where it is supposed to be. The slightest intentional human disruption will lead to disorder and make the spirits very unhappy."

"It's like a more eerie version of the butterfly effect," Clint told her.

"What's that?" Tanna wanted to know.

"There's a theory stateside that even the interruption of a butterfly flapping its wings can have a ripple effect and cause devastating changes throughout eternity."

Tanna studied his face for a moment. "That's heavy." Then she eyed them both before continuing, "Can I tell you two something?"

They both nodded as Tanna leaned in and lowered her voice. "This very resort was built on sacred ceremonial ground. My *tutu* keeps imploring me to quit this job. I could tell you stories from guests that would make you want to check out right now." A silence settled in the air between them. Suddenly, Tanna straightened. "Anyway, can I get you anything else?" she asked, indicating Clint's empty glass.

"No, thanks."

Great. Just great. Rita grabbed her still-full goblet and downed the glass of wine she suddenly decided she wanted. As if she didn't have enough on her mind. Now she had to worry that she may have inadvertently jinxed Lizzie's wedding.

A bubble of laughter crawled up her throat as she realized how silly that notion was. Curses. Spirits. She was essentially a scientist by trade, trained as an animal veterinarian. She didn't believe in anything so fanciful.

But a nagging sensation ran over the back of her neck as they stood to leave. She could have sworn the breeze picked up just then, enough to whip a nasty gust of sand into her face.

Rita punched her pillow for what had to be the hundredth time in the past two hours. The digital clock next to her bed read 3:10 a.m. Would she ever get any sleep tonight? As exhausted as she was, she desperately needed it. But what her muscles were craving, a sound night of rest, her mind just didn't seem to be in the mood for. And her mind could be quite stubborn.

Rather than allowing her to succumb to much-needed slumber, her mind insisted on replaying the scenes of the day on a repeat loop. Clint's smile as he pulled her off the cliff to jump with him. The way he pointed out the glorious mountains in the distance during the drive. How he'd held her in the cave. Each moment of remembrance sent a tingle of awareness down her spine.

Oh, and there was also that thoughtful, kind gesture he'd made to his sister when he'd sent her room service after the fight. Not to mention, all that he'd shared with her about the difficulties he and Lizzie had endured growing up.

She had to stop thinking about him.

Only when she forced her mind away from the enigmatic man who seemed to be haunting her thoughts, it turned to a disturbing mishmash of angry spirits and a crying dead princess.

Get a grip, already.

She tossed onto her back with a frustrated sigh and stared at the blinking light of the fire alarm on the ceiling. Tessa was breathing evenly in the twin bed next to hers. Surprisingly, her roommate had made it in alone and at a decent hour last night. The epic fight between bride and groom that everyone witnessed in the lobby no doubt cast a pall on more than one partygoer's plans.

She counted seventy-five blinks on the alarm, then forced herself to close her eyes. If sleep was going to elude her all night, then she'd just have to stare at the inside of her eyelids for a while. Only now she could see the blinking light in her head, so she started counting again. Some people counted sheep. She got enough of animals during her waking hours. She found other things to count. She made it to eighty this time when she felt the air shift at the foot of her bed. Now she was disrupting her roommate's sleep with her constant tossing and turning.

"Sorry, Tessa. Bad case of insomnia. It's why I'm moving around so much and rustling the sheets."

But the responding mumble from Tessa came from the other side of the room. Where she was apparently still in bed. Rita's eyelids flew open. A shadow moved from the foot of her bed to the side and then to the sliding glass door of the balcony.

Rita's mouth went dry and her heart pounded in her chest. She was not imagining it. Clicking on the small night-light above the headboard, she bolted upright.

Nothing.

There was no one there.

Rita blew out a long sigh of relief. Talk about getting a grip. She was letting all the ghost stories get to her. There was no such thing as a crying princess spirit. There was no such thing as a vengeful one who wanted to keep all his rocks on his beach. Really, she had to stop taking everything people told her to heart. Also, putting an end to any kind of late-night drinking would probably be wise, as well.

Throwing the covers off, she rose out of bed to get a glass of water from the bathroom. A crumpled piece of fabric lay on the floor by the bathroom door. She kicked it aside before realizing what it was.

But it couldn't be.

With dread, Rita bent to pick up the item to make sure. Her mouth went dry when she saw what it was she held. Her jean shorts. The ones with the rock in the pocket. She was one hundred percent certain she'd thrown those in the closet atop her other worn clothing when she'd walked in this evening. In fact, the rock had been completely forgotten after the emotional tug of the fight between Lizzie and Jonathon. She hadn't given it a second thought until all the talk of curses and spirits.

The added weight of the fabric told her it was still in there. Was she losing her mind? Had she pulled it out and forgotten somehow? There had to be a logical explanation.

She'd never been one to entertain superstition. But her father had grown up believing in various gods and guiding spirits. He wasn't terribly traditional but he'd definitely carried over some beliefs with him.

Even as a child, she'd always scoffed at his stories, along with her mother. They were both convinced that he couldn't really believe all the things he was spouting. It all seemed the stuff of fairy tales and lore, though Papa insisted it was all real.

In a stunned daze, Rita made her way back to bed. The night-light was going to stay on for the remainder of the night. One thing was certain, she had lost all hope of getting any sleep.

CHAPTER SEVEN

CLINT FOUND IT impossible to sleep.

Now as a result of a restless, frustrating night he'd started his jog ridiculously early. The term *predawn* came to mind. Rita. She'd been all he could think about. The whole day spent with her yesterday was magical. One he'd never forget. But she'd gone suddenly quiet after their nightcap. He had been about to suggest a walk along the beach when she'd abruptly bidden him goodnight and then practically run to the elevator.

Was it something he'd said?

He hadn't meant to get into all that about his grandmother and the loss of his parents. Those weren't topics he normally entertained or liked to talk about. Not with anyone. But the more he got to know Rita, the more he felt able to open up. Even about his childhood. And she'd seemed genuinely interested, asked him to confide in her. Which had been far too easy. He'd never felt so comfortable around a woman, so at ease with just being himself.

But something had definitely spooked her at the end. Served him right. The past was better left behind where it belonged.

Then there was the worry about his sister. He'd not heard from her at all after that little display in the lobby other than a quick text.

Thank you for the wine and chocolate, big brother. Just need some time alone. Time to think.

Women. He would never understand them. It was why he was going to stay single for as long as he could. Perhaps even as long as he lived. A set of dreamy dark chocolate eyes framed by long lashes flashed into his mind. He pounded the sand even harder.

By the time he made it back to the entrance of the hotel lobby, he'd only hammered out a fraction of his frustration. But it was better than nothing. The resort was still quiet. Only maintenance and servicemen were up and about.

So he figured he was seeing things when he spotted Rita at the outside bellhop stand. Clint squinted against the early sun rays. Yeah, it was definitely her. What in the world was she doing out here at this time of morning?

One way to find out.

The bellhop was typing something out for her on his handheld tablet when Clint tapped her on the shoulder. She jumped and clapped a hand to her chest.

"Clint. What are you doing here?"

He made a show of looking down at his work-out clothes and lifted the cell phone in his hands, then pointed to the wireless earbuds in his ears.

"Right. How was your run?"

He ignored that. He also tried hard to ignore her shapely, toned legs in the black capri leggings she was wearing. Or the way the white tank beneath her jean jacket came up just above her cleavage.

"Going somewhere?"

"As a matter of fact, I am. I was going to try to text Lizzie later. Both to check in and to see how she was doing."

She was going to text Lizzie. Had no intention of contacting him. Why that thought stung was beyond him. She certainly didn't need to okay her whereabouts with him. Though it would have been nice.

"She told me last night she just wanted some time to think. Alone. Where?"

"Huh?"

"Where are you planning to go?"

She bit down on her lower lip. "I'd rather not say."

The bellhop's gaze bounced from one to the other, as if he was watching a slow, yet gripping, tennis match.

Clint was in no mood for this. Between concern for his sister, worry that they might end up canceling this whole soiree and trying to figure out the rapidly changing mood of the woman before him, Clint figured he was swiftly reaching his outer limits.

"I have a real problem with that," he declared.

Rita blinked at him. "I beg your pardon?"

"I have a real issue with your refusal to tell me where you're going."

Anger flashed through her eyes. Rather than heed the warning, Clint stepped in closer.

"You have an issue with my refusal to tell you something that's none of your business in the first place?"

"That's where you're wrong. I think it's plenty my business."

Her chin lifted with defiance. "I utterly fail to see how."

"Let me explain then," he said, knowing he was being a bit of a heel given his tone and his wording. But he couldn't seem to help himself. She was about to take off in the wee hours of the morning without a word to anyone. Her plan only to drop a text to his sister later. A sister who was plenty distracted and might not even be looking at her phone for countless reasons. "I'm responsible for this event and for the wedding party here to attend it."

"You certainly aren't responsible for me."

"You're here for this wedding aren't you? The one we're having for my sister?"

She leaned back and crossed her arms in front of her chest. "I'm sorry. Does that somehow mean I have given up my free will?"

"What? Of course not. I'd just rather have an idea where my guests may be." *And, in her case, feel assured that they're safe and secure.*

The bellhop cleared his throat behind them. "Ms. Paul, if you'll excuse me. I'm afraid the only cars available are smaller hatchbacks. I wouldn't recommend one of those on the drive to Hana.

Would you like me to see if there's a tour I can book you on?"

Rita threw the man a hard glare. "No, thank you. That won't be necessary."

Clint wanted to shake the man's hand. Now he knew where she was going. He just couldn't guess why.

"You enjoy the tour that much?" Clint asked. "Have to go back the next day?"

"Don't be silly. I only want to get to one spot."

"What spot could possibly be so intriguing?"

But she ignored him. "I'll take one of the hatchbacks," she told the bellhop, who now seemed a little afraid, judging by the way he took a step backward.

Was she nuts? She was going to try to drive that rugged terrain in a hatchback? Some of those roads were downright treacherous. Never mind the winding curves that required the stability of a much larger vehicle.

The thought made him shudder. He knew first-hand how a seemingly frivolous decision during a trip could alter one's fate. His parents had made just such a decision and it had cost them their lives.

"Right away, miss." He picked up the tablet.

"What are you doing?" he demanded to know. "Don't you remember all those cars we saw rotted out at the bottom as we drove on some of those mountain roads? What are you thinking?"

"I'm thinking I'm an excellent driver. Please go forward with the car," she directed the bellhop once more.

Clint held up a hand to stop him. "Hold off, please."

Rita practically jumped on her heels in protest. "I am trying to secure a car which I need to get somewhere. You have no say in this."

"Just stop," he told her before she could continue the takedown she was so prepared for. Of him. "That won't be necessary."

Drawing a steadying breath, he focused back on her face. Her lips were pursed, her eyes held a hardened glint. He knew determination when he saw it. She was going to her destination whether he wanted her to or not. "I always make sure to rent a car when I travel. Usually a late-model SUV. I've done so this time. It's available to you if you want it."

That took the wind out of her sails. She visibly relaxed and lowered her shoulders.

"But I'm going to ask to come with you," he

added before she relaxed too much. "I'd really rather you not travel that route alone."

"What if I say no? Will you revoke the offer of your car?"

"No, it's still yours if you want it."

A slight softening showed behind her eyes but then swiftly disappeared at his next words. "I'll just follow you if I have to."

Her lips tightened into a thin line once more. "How? You've given me your car."

He shrugged. "Guess I'll have to take one of those death-trap hatchbacks. Just hope and pray I don't plummet to the bottom of Mount Name-I-Can't-Pronounce to my untimely and tragic death." Hard to believe he could joke about such a thing, but there it was.

A smile tugged at the corners of her mouth. He could see her lips trembling in an attempt to control it from fully blossoming. Throwing her hands up, she rolled her eyes. "Fine. Come with me if you insist. But you're probably just going to laugh and call me all kinds of foolish." She looked him over, from his sweaty forehead to the grains of sand on his running shoes. "I suppose you're going to want to get cleaned up first."

"If it's not too much of an imposition," he said with mock seriousness, then bowed.

Rita simply shook her head slowly, then turned on her heel and walked back into the lobby of the hotel. Taking a moment to breathe a sigh of relief, he gave the bellhop a nod of thanks. The other man wiggled his eyebrows at him, his meaning clear. Yeah, Clint had his hands full. With another silent nod of agreement, he turned to follow her.

When he thought about how much of a coincidental fluke it was that he'd run into her in the first place, he cursed out loud. Thank the heavens he'd started his jog early. Or she could very well have been puttering up a mountain right now in a rackety small hatchback.

Whatever her reasons for wanting this so badly, he couldn't even venture to guess. One could only hope they were good ones. But he couldn't help but wonder which one of them was really the fool in all this.

Clint keyed the necessary information into the GPS and pulled the midsize Range Rover onto the road leading out of the resort. He and Rita had decided to take turns driving and he'd won the coin toss to determine who'd go first. Or maybe he'd lost, he couldn't even be sure. He didn't seem to know which way was up when it came to this particular woman.

So why did he find that intriguing when he ought to be downright annoyed about it instead?

He slid his gaze to the passenger seat where she sat next to him, fiercely studying the view from the window. Her legs were crossed, one shapely calve over the other. He'd touched her enough times to know her skin was soft and smooth. Her legs would probably feel that way too under the palm of his hand.

He gripped the steering wheel tighter and pulled his attention to the road.

She was completely different from any woman he'd previously dated. He had thought he preferred blondes, but he seemed to be enamored with her dark silky hair. She wore it up in some type of loose bun at the moment; wispy tendrils framed her face. The effect lent a soft, angelic quality to her features.

Whereas most of his previous dates were curvy, Rita was lithe and toned. And unlike Maxine, his most recent terminated relationship, Rita wore very minimal makeup.

"Are we heading the same way we did yesterday?" she asked, pulling him out of his somewhat inappropriate musings about her body and her hair.

"Yes. But you're eventually going to have to tell me what our ultimate destination is. Unless you plan on blindfolding me at some point."

That notion brought up all sorts of inappropriate thoughts dancing in his brain. He made himself focus on the road; they hadn't even left the city yet. It was going to be another long day. For some reason, that idea didn't fill him with dread the way it should have.

She slowly folded the map, rubbed her forehead. "I'm trying to rectify a mistake I made yesterday. Or think I made. I don't even know."

That made no sense whatsoever. He waited for her to continue.

"I took something I shouldn't have."

She couldn't mean what he thought she meant. The idea was a preposterous one. "Are you saying you took something from one of the souvenir shops? Without paying for it?"

She gasped and shifted in her seat to stare at him, her mouth agape. "What? No! How could you even think that?"

"I didn't really. I mean—I don't know what I mean. I'm just trying to understand what's happening."

"I didn't steal anything, Clint. I'm not a thief!" she declared on a huff.

"Then what are you talking about? Why are we retracing our route from yesterday?"

"I took a rock, okay? I need to get back to Black Sand Beach."

He couldn't have heard her right. A rock?

She blew out a breath. "I think it's my fault Lizzie and Jonathon are fighting."

Okay. Maybe Rita *had* hit her head when they'd jumped off that cliff and he'd missed it. Clint thought about turning around and finding the nearest medical clinic instead of continuing on their current route. But she'd been pretty coherent the rest of the day after that.

"Because the spirits are angry," she added.

Angry spirits…? Understanding slowly dawned as he recalled the waitress from last night and her dire warnings about curses and spirits. Rita was staring at him with expectation.

"Huh" was all he could muster.

"That's it?" she asked. "That's all you have to say to what I just told you?"

"You think you picked up a cursed rock and now you want to return it. In case it has something to do with the sudden threat to Lizzie's nuptials. Does that about summarize it?"

She nodded slowly, still hadn't shut her mouth completely. And what a luscious, beckoning mouth it was. Full lips just slightly pink above a rounded, feminine jaw.

"Yes," she replied. "It's why I want to go back to Black Sand Beach."

Now, why was it so hard for her to have told him that? Honestly, he couldn't figure her out at all.

"All right. Let's hope we make good time. It looks cloudier today than yesterday. We might be a bit chilled."

She gave her head a shake. "You're not even going to try to tell me I'm being silly? That going through all this trouble for a supposed curse is a downright waste of time?"

"Why would I do that?"

She let out a small chuckle. "I know you're not saying you believe it, that something like a lifted rock can have any kind of effect on a wedding." She rubbed her brow. "Sheesh, when I say it out loud, it sounds even more outlandish."

He shrugged. "I know you believe it. That's enough."

"It is?"

"It is for me." He turned onto the Hana High-way.

The thing was, Rita wasn't even sure if she did believe in the curse. In fact, she was almost cer- tain that she didn't give it much credence at all.

She just didn't want to risk it. Not after what- ever it was that she'd seen last night. And she still couldn't explain how her shorts had ended up out of the closet and on the floor.

She fingered the object in question inside her jacket pocket. The rock felt smooth and sleek under her skin. As small as a pebble. Hard to believe it could cause any kind of trouble. Well, it was too late to back out now. If Clint thought she was crazy, he was doing a good job of keep- ing that to himself.

The ride went by in comfortable silence. For the most part anyway. It certainly wasn't com- fortable that she was so very aware of him.

He'd changed into navy-blue sailing shorts and a white V-neck tee that brought out his newly tanned skin. A silver-and-gold watch clasped on his right wrist had the most complicated face on it she'd ever seen, with three different dials and four hands. His hair was still wet and combed back to reveal his strong, square jaw.

Even dressed island casual, the man looked like he could grace the cover of *Executive Today* magazine.

Rita forced her attention to the road ahead. It was indeed quite curvy, perilously close to the edge in several spots. But Clint was effortlessly navigating the car in such a smooth way, her stomach hadn't dipped once. So unlike the ride yesterday.

"Are you getting tired of driving yet?" she asked, hoping the answer would be no. For all her protests earlier, she was quite enjoying being able to sit back and enjoy the scenery. No way she'd ever share that bit with him though.

"I think I'm good. No real good spots to stop anyway. Not for a while."

Nodding, Rita turned to stare at the sapphire-blue water beyond the mountain road they were driving on. She'd tried to stay angry, she really had, about the way he'd commandeered the whole endeavor. But how upset could she really be? He hadn't made fun of her. In fact, he hadn't so much as even smirked. He'd provided her with a steady and reliable car for the trip, and spared her from having to make the ride on her own.

Even if he had been a little domineering in the process.

No one was perfect, right?

Between her overbearing father and control-loving ex-husband, it was been-there-done-that as far as she was concerned. Regardless of his well-intentioned motivations, Clint had definitely shown a similar quality earlier today when he'd found her at the bellhop podium.

Moot point. It wasn't like she was committing herself for life to the man. She had just accepted his gracious offer to assist her with her mission. Nothing more.

With what seemed like great time, they finally pulled up to a gravel road. A large wooden sign at the entry said Wai'anapanapa State Park. Rita felt like months had gone by since they'd been here. Hard to believe it had been less than a day. So much had happened since. Clint pulled into one of the parking spots and they both got out of the car. Except, where Rita's limbs felt sore and stiff, Clint seemed to be able to bounce out of the SUV and easily stride to where she stood. Athletic and agile.

"All right. Let's go get uncursed," he said.

She tried to hide her trepidation. What if it didn't work that way? What if the spirits were unforgiving types that didn't care about attempts at restitution after the fact?

She'd never forgive herself if Lizzie and Jonathon broke up for good and there was even the slightest possibility she'd caused it. Even indirectly.

"Let's go." She started walking to the concrete steps that led down to the beach area. "I'll show you where I picked it up."

Clint had been right about today's weather being cloudier and more windy. These waves were definitely harsher than yesterday's. Angry water pounded on the boulders and sent splashes of foam high into the air. A mist of salt water fanned her face when they reached the bottom step.

"I picked it up in the cave," she told him and navigated around two jeans-clad teenagers taking selfies.

"Guess I shouldn't have pulled you in there yesterday," Clint responded.

But he *had* pulled her in. And they'd been merely inches apart. And she couldn't forget that she'd actually imagined him kissing her, had wanted him to.

"I'm the one who picked up the rock."

"Which is why we're here." He led her toward the crashing waves and to the mouth of the cave in a replay of yesterday. It occurred to her that today there'd be no one to yell at them to come out, to tell them they needed to leave. A shiver of apprehension traveled up her spine. Or maybe it was more anticipation.

She stepped inside and he followed closely behind her. "I guess I should try to put it exactly where I found it on the ground. Or as close as possible."

"Right. So he can be reunited with all his little pebble friends."

"Ha ha." Rita bent down and gently deposited the rock, then straightened. Already, a sense of calm and relief settled over her. Superstition or not, she definitely felt a sense of unburdening.

"Ready?" Clint asked.

She nodded. "Seems anticlimactic somehow."

"You were expecting drama? Or perhaps that

the spirits would descend all of a sudden and bestow you with thanks and praise?"

She smiled. "It's the least they could do, you know. They've put us through a lot of trouble."

He fished out his phone. Looked back up at her, eyes wide with shock. "You're not gonna believe this. Lizzie just texted that she and Jonathon have completely made up. Just this very moment."

Rita felt her jaw drop with disbelief. "Oh, my God! You're kidding?"

He waited a beat, then grinned. "Yeah, I am." He slid his phone back in his pocket. "I'm not even getting cell reception."

He was teasing her! Of all times. She reached over and gave him a useless shove. "That was mean."

The laughter died in her throat at his expression. Clint's gaze dropped to where her hand touched his shoulder. To her surprise, he wrapped his fingers around her own. His skin felt warm, strong against hers.

"You almost fell yesterday in here. Remember?" he asked, his voice near a whisper.

Rita's mouth went dry. If he only knew. Yes, she remembered. She'd been thinking about it ever since. The way he'd grabbed her to keep her upright. The solid wall of muscle against her back as he'd held her steady against him. "Guess I should thank you for that too."

His gaze fell to her mouth. "Maybe you can show me."

There it was. A clear invitation. All pretense gone.

And he'd made sure it would be her decision. The ball was fully in her court.

What would he taste like? How would his lips feel against hers? She'd thought so often about kissing him before, when she was merely a besotted coed with a crush. It had never occurred to her back then that she would ever get the opportunity. Yet, here it was. As if she was in some sort of fairy tale or dream. Their time together on Maui had only served to heighten her attraction. She'd grown increasingly more aware of him every moment they spent together. All too often on this trip, her imagination had created scenarios of the two of them together. Intimately. Scenarios, through some miracle, exactly like the one she found herself in now.

Rita had the distinct impression reality would be even better than the products of her imagination. She could guess what he would taste like: masculine and bold. His lips would be firm against hers, just as she'd so often dreamed.

It would be so easy to find out once and for all, to just lean into him and take him up on his tempting offer.

But could she? Could she tune out all the warnings, the red flags? All her life, she'd tried so hard to do what was expected of her, what others told her was the right thing. This one time, did she have the courage to simply do exactly what she wanted?

And she so desperately wanted.

Clint's breath caught as he watched Rita's inner struggle. He knew what she wanted; her eyes had clouded with desire. He had no doubt about that. Whether she would act on it was a completely different question. He willed himself not to move so much as a muscle. As badly as he wanted to lean into her and finally take those lush, tempting lips with his own, the next step would have to be hers. Whatever happened next between them had to be completely on her own terms.

It was only fair.

Not that he was trying to be honorable. The only real honorable thing to do would be to walk away, if he was being honest. Relationships weren't his thing. Not long-term ones. Fallon men couldn't be trusted with real commitment. History told that it never went well. Between his parents' fatal accident and his grandfather's self-inflicted untimely death, Clint determined long ago that he was never meant to be a family man.

He wouldn't lead someone like Rita on. But he could no longer deny his attraction. Nor hide it.

"I don't think that's such a good idea," she finally answered with a breathy rasp. A bolt of disappointment stabbed through his center. He felt the loss like a physical blow. A blow that wasn't the least lessened by the fact that she was right. Of course she was.

"It's not that I don't want to."

Well, that was something at least. It helped, though not much.

"It's just..." She thrust a hand through the hair at her crown. "I'm not sure exactly who I am at this very moment in time. I know it sounds silly."

Clint wanted desperately to wrap her tight in his arms, to kiss away the tension and angst clear in every muscle in her face. "It doesn't sound silly, Rita."

"I wish I could explain."

She didn't get a chance to try. A boisterous family of four appeared in the entryway and made their way inside.

"Ooh, spooky," the teenage girl said, her eyes glancing around the dark cave walls.

"You're a wuss" came the reply from her smaller brother, who stepped around her to go farther inside.

Clint cursed under his breath while Rita smiled politely at the intruders.

"We should go," he told Rita and gently took her by the elbow. "It's getting crowded in here," he added in a lower voice only she could hear.

"You all have a good day," the woman said pleasantly as they stepped out.

It occurred to Clint just how they must have looked, like a besotted couple who'd been interrupted as they stole a private moment in a beachside cavern.

So far from the truth it caused a pang in his gut.

"We've traveled quite a distance. It would be a shame just to turn around and go back." Clint opened the car door for Rita and waited as she crawled inside. It wasn't easy acting like nothing had just happened between them before the family had come in. Although, technically, nothing actually *had* happened.

Entering the car, he shut his door a little too hard. Rita winced slightly next to him.

"What did you have in mind?" she asked.

"A few stops I've heard about that the driver didn't take us to yesterday. Off the beaten path, so to speak. Are you hungry?"

Her stomach answered for her. As soon as he asked the question, he heard a soft grumbling coming from her midsection.

"Take a guess," she said in a giggle.

"There's supposedly a roadside hut that serves the best banana bread on the island. Or so I've been told."

"Sold. But only if it's my treat." She seemed genuinely excited. He hoped at least part of that came from not wanting their private little outing to end just yet. Maybe he was fooling himself. She was simply hungry. Still, he'd take it.

"It's a deal." He put the car in gear and began to drive.

Within minutes, they'd reached the stand and were handed tinfoil-wrapped loaves of aromatic bread that made his mouth water. Rita began tearing at the foil.

"Uh-uh." He stopped her by placing his hand on hers. "Not yet."

She glared at him. "Why not? I want my lunch."

Her outrage made him laugh. "Patience. We can eat it at the next stop."

She reluctantly lowered the bread. "We're still off the beaten path then?"

"Let's go." He'd been thinking about taking her to this next stop all day. Hoped it would live up to expectations. From what he'd been told, the spot was a well-kept secret among the locals who didn't want it overrun with campy tourists the way the state properties usually were.

Rita seemed the type who would appreciate a place like that.

He had his answer when they reached the isolated beach about half an hour later. She gasped as he pulled up along the side of the road and put the car in gear. Before he could turn off the ignition, she'd already exited and started running toward the small stretch of beach.

"Oh, Clint!"

"What do you think?"

"It's pink! I've never seen anything like it. The sand is actually pink! I thought the black sand was impressive."

Before them lay a crystal-blue pool of water surrounded by sand the likes of which he'd never seen before. Rita was partly right as far as he was concerned. He'd describe the color as more of a ruby red, depending on where the light hit it.

"This is otherworldly." She bent down and scooped some of the sand into her palm before letting it slowly sift through her fingers.

"I figured we'd have our banana bread lunch here. Make a picnic out of it."

The smile she flashed him gave him the response he wanted. It also nearly took his breath away. An almost giddy sense of pleasure hit him at how happy she was to be here.

What a schoolboy with a crush he was acting like.

They sat down on a large boulder between the road and water and began to eat.

"Looks like we have company." Clint swallowed the bite he had in his mouth as a large lanky dog jogged toward them. It stopped about six inches away and started sniffing at the food. Clint's food to be more accurate. Rita had impressed him by finishing first.

"Hey, baby." She stood and held her hand to the dog's nose to sniff.

"Is it a stray?"

"I don't think so. No collar but it seems taken care of. Well-fed, no signs of emaciation."

Right. She was a vet after all. The dog licked her finger, then turned back to Clint, eyeing the bread again.

He pulled the loaf back. "This is mine."

Rita squatted in front of the animal. "Are you lost, girl? Let's take a look at you." Placing her fingers along the dog's jaw, she slowly pried its mouth open.

Clint stopped chewing. "Um…is that wise?"

She ignored the question. "Teeth look good. Relatively clean for what I'd guess is her age. She seems to be some type of pit bull–mix breed. Definitely some other terrier in there too."

"So she's not lost?"

Rita looked up to glance at the road behind them. "There are some houses back there. I'm guessing she's just out wandering."

"I think she smelled banana and came looking." He could have sworn the dog actually nodded at that statement. Then it lifted a paw and dropped it onto Clint's knee.

There was barely one morsel left.

"She likes you," Rita declared, clearly laughing at his displeasure.

"She wants my lunch."

Again, he could swear the dog was nodding. He suddenly felt guilty. "Should I give her some?"

Rita seemed to think. "Probably not. It shouldn't harm her but it is pretty sweet. Sugar sometimes upsets their digestive tract."

Guilt evaporated, Clint popped the last piece of bread into his mouth, then leaned over to rub the dog's head. "Sorry, pal. You heard the doc."

He got a sharp bark in response. "Hey, you should be thanking me. I just spared you an upset tummy."

"And diarrhea," Rita added.

Well, now things were getting romantic. The dog gave him one more derisive look, then dropped its paw and started to walk away. Rita followed for a few feet and watched it cross the road.

"She seems to be heading toward that brown house at the turn," she told him over her shoulder.

Sure enough, they both watched as their former visitor walked through the yard and jumped through what appeared to be a puppy door by the side of the house.

Clint heard Rita's sigh of relief. He had the distinct feeling she would have followed that dog until she made sure it had a home and had reached it safely.

"What a cutie," she said and returned to her spot next to him on the boulder. "Do you have any pets?"

Clint shook his head. "I'm never home long enough. The poor thing would starve. I imagine you have a few."

"Not right now. Jay had allergies. He'd react even to the hypoallergenic breeds. So we never bothered to get one."

"Couldn't you have gotten one of those hairless cats or something?"

She bit out a short laugh. "Sphynx cats? Believe it or not, people have reactions to those too."

"My sister wanted one of those, though I'll never understand why. I personally think they look like deflated balloons. With a face." He picked a small pink pebble, thought about throwing it into the water and dropped it back down. In case the curse applied to more than just Black Sand Beach.

And since when did he give any credence to curses and such? He hardly recognized himself on this trip. Now here he was sitting on a magical beach with the most beautiful, alluring woman and so far they'd talked about canine diarrhea and hairless cats.

"But she never got one," he continued. "We didn't have any pets growing up."

"Oh?"

"My grandmother wouldn't allow it. She said she had enough on her hands being strapped with two teenagers to bring up at her late stage in life. Wouldn't budge even though we swore we'd be the ones taking care of any animal she'd let us get." He stared off into the water. "Heck, Lizzie would have settled for a goldfish."

"That's too bad. I think pets serve to teach children a great deal. Particularly a good sense of responsibility."

"Other than that, Grams was all about responsibility." Especially when it came to him. "Our grandmother made no secret of the fact that she'd disapproved of my parents' marriage," he added, not quite certain why he was ready to share so much with her. These were things he'd never spoken out loud about with anyone. Not even Lizzie. "Almost seemed to take it as a personal affront.

I got the impression I was somehow supposed to make up for their transgressions to her."

She touched his knee in sympathy. An electric current shot through from the point of contact straight through his chest.

"That's a lot to process for a teenage boy."

"Past history." He shrugged, ready to change the subject. "So what was the last pet you owned?"

"My parents always had one or two dogs. This past year was the first time in my life I didn't have an animal to come home to."

"Good thing you get enough animal contact through your work then, huh?"

She bit her bottom lip, looked out over the water. "I'm not practicing right now."

Whatever the reason, she didn't seem happy about it. He got the impression her sabbatical wasn't by choice. Not her choice, in any case.

"Why's that?"

"Long story. Jay asked me to quit when we first got married. He wanted to focus on a family. I'd only taken the job to make him happy anyway."

"I don't understand."

"My original goal out of college was to try to start my own practice, set up shop somewhere. Or to work with one of the local animal shelters.

But both those options would have taken countless grueling hours and total commitment. Jay wasn't too keen on that idea. I let him convince me to try for a clinic instead. He had some help from my parents in the convincing department. They'd never understood my career choice anyway." Her laugh was not a genuine one. "Neither my mother or father could figure out why I'd want to go through all that schooling and training and not become an actual doctor." She used air quotes to emphasize the last two words.

Clint continued to play with the sand at his feet. Staying silent seemed to be the best course of action right now. To just let her continue.

"Anyway, I ended up at a chain practice where they controlled everything from my schedule to the length of my patient visits."

"That doesn't sound like a good fit for you."

"It wasn't. It got to the point where I started spending more time filling out forms to prove profit contribution to the clinic than I did actually treating pets. So when Jay asked me to quit…"

"You quit to make him happy."

"I guess I did."

"And now?"

She tucked a strand of hair behind her ear. "What do you mean?"

He thought his meaning should be obvious, but she was looking at him expectantly. "What's stopping you now from going after that original goal?"

She blinked, then looked away into the distance. "I don't know if I even have the same goals anymore. A lot has happened since I got my degree."

"Sure it has. You've gained even more experience in your field." He thought of the way she'd handled the wandering dog just now, the pure contentment and energy in her eyes as she tended to it. "You're clearly good at what you do."

She smiled. "I suppose. I just don't know if I have it in me any longer to pursue such grand endeavors. Right now, I just need to settle into a quiet, comfortable routine."

"Sounds a bit boring."

Her chuckle was half-hearted. "I could do with a little boring at this point in time."

More likely, she was scared. Based on the little bit she'd confided, her decisions had been questioned so often and so thoroughly, she was probably hesitant about making any more major ones.

Clint would keep all that to himself. Who was he to try to analyze her choices?

"Yet one more thing to figure out, I guess," she added, not tearing her gaze away from the horizon.

He didn't say anything else, though he desperately wanted to. He simply reached for the hand she still had on his knee and gave it a tight squeeze. They sat in silence for long enough that he actually lost track of the time. Five minutes or an hour could have gone by before Rita spoke again.

"Clint." The way she said his name made his heart hammer.

"Yeah?"

"I've changed my mind."

He lifted an eyebrow in question. Then sucked in a breath at her next words.

"I would like you to kiss me. In fact, I'd like it very much."

Rita couldn't recall ever being so bold. She'd asked before she could let herself think too much longer about doing so. And now she couldn't think at all.

Clint's kiss was gentle at first, like a soft breeze

on a warm summer evening. But then something turned. He took her by the waist, pulled her closer, her body tight up against his. His mouth grew demanding, delving deeper and asking for more. She was oh, so ready to give it. Shivers ran down her whole body, desire racked her core. She'd never felt such intense longing for a man, simply from his kiss.

A thrill shot through her chest at the knowledge that he wanted her, as well. There was no doubt, not given the way he held her, the way he was plundering her mouth with his own.

So this was what true passion felt like, what all the books and movies and love songs were always referring to. All these years, she'd had no idea until this very moment. With this one man.

Her hands moved up his arms to his shoulders. She wanted him closer somehow, would never get close enough. Her heart hammered in her chest as she molded her body against his. Nothing in her past dreams could have prepared her for the reality of being in his arms, tasting him like this. Her fantasies hadn't done him justice. He was making her burn through to her very soul. An exquisite, enticing burn she'd never get enough of. He tasted like sin and pure masculinity. And banana bread.

That random thought served to pull her out of the spell. Enough to let all the warning cries in. Abruptly, she made herself tear away from his grasp. The loss felt like a bucket of cold water splashed into her face.

She shouldn't be doing this. Couldn't be doing this.

She'd made too many mistakes in these past few years. It would take her years to recover from them.

She couldn't make another one by losing her heart to Clint. There would be no recovering from that.

Clint Fallon wasn't the type of man a girl got over. Ever.

CHAPTER EIGHT

THE RIDE BACK was mostly silent save for the luau music playing on the radio. She'd noticed Clint had gradually turned up the volume higher and higher, as if it somehow refuted the lack of conversation between them. Neither one seemed to know what to say to each other.

Rita felt like a wound-up ball of emotion by the time they returned to the resort and went their separate ways. Her distraction was the reason it took her a minute to realize what she'd walked in on after she opened the door to her room and switched on the light.

She quickly shut if off again as soon as her eyes adjusted and she realized what she was seeing.

"Rita!" Tessa's surprised voice shouted across the room from her bed, immediately followed by the low rumble of a man's chuckle. It appeared Tessa and the groomsman had taken their friendship to the next level.

"It's o-okay," Rita stammered and tried to walk

quickly backward out the door. Her jacket pocket caught on the doorknob and yanked her to a halt.

Tessa appeared at the door, wrapped in a sheet. Which had to mean the groomsman wasn't covered at the moment. She made sure to quickly avert her gaze.

"I'm really sorry, Rita. I guess I wasn't expecting you back. You've been gone all day."

"We were exploring the island."

Tessa gave a nod. "With Clint, right? You've both been gone. I just assumed…"

Rita could guess what she'd assumed. "It's okay. I didn't mean to interrupt." It didn't quite feel right that she was the one apologizing but somehow she felt the need.

Tessa blew a tuft of hair off her forehead. "I mean," she said, dropping her voice to a whisper, "Rob and I have been really hitting it off, you know. It's like—I've never felt so attracted to someone. Hasn't that ever happened to you?"

She didn't know how to answer that. It had happened, so very recently. It *was* happening. And she didn't know how to cope with it.

"I'm happy for you," Rita blurted out, not even sure if it was an appropriate response for this moment.

"Thanks. I guess I kinda figured you'd sort of be occupied too."

An image flashed through her mind of exactly what Tessa was referring to. In that picture, it was her and Clint wrapped up in each other under the sheets in a dark room.

She sucked in a breath and forced her mind to focus on Tessa's face.

"Listen, it's okay. You guys...uh...you guys have fun."

Tessa squealed a small laugh. "Oh, we are."

"How about you just drop me a text when it's safe for me to return?"

Tessa leaned over to give her a one-armed hug, the other hand holding tight to the sheet. "Thanks, Rita! You're the best. I'll call you as soon as... Well, you know."

Rita backed away into the hallway as the door shut. The squeal she heard from Tessa in the next instant sounded nothing like the one from before.

Making her way to the ground-floor lounge, she settled on the couch and adjusted a cushion behind her, trying to get comfortable. She almost envied her roommate. To be that bold, to feel that liberated had to be so freeing in so many ways. Tessa obviously didn't give much thought to long-term ramifications. While planning for the future had been a constant theme in the way Rita lived her life. Look how that had turned out. Rita sighed and closed her eyes, willing for at least a few moments of sleep before she could go back to the room.

Tessa's text never came.

He'd become quite the wanderer in Hawaii. Clint made his way down the stairs and past the lobby. He'd gotten tired of tossing and turning, trying to get to sleep. It wasn't early in the evening but it certainly wasn't late by any means. He and Rita had gotten back less than three hours ago.

He couldn't stop thinking about her. Or the way she'd kissed him.

More than that, she'd opened up to him. Though it had been difficult to hear about her former husband. Just the thought that she'd belonged to another man not so long ago made him want to punch a wall. How utterly Neanderthal-like. He wasn't proud of his reaction.

Rita and her ex sounded like two completely different people, totally incompatible. Rita was warm, genuine and fully appreciative of everything around her. Her ex-husband seemed the stoic and serious type. He blew out a frustrated breath. What did he know about it? He'd never even met the man. In fact, he'd never felt such a strong dislike for someone he'd never laid eyes on.

He halted in his tracks as he approached the sitting area by the ground-floor lounge. Great. Now he was starting to see her everywhere. That couldn't really be her sprawled out on one of the couches.

He drew closer to find it was indeed her.

"Rita?" He gently tapped her on the shoulder. Once, twice. Nothing. Leaning in, he gave her arm a gentle squeeze. Finally, she started to stir.

"Clint?"

"Yeah. Hey, what are you doing here? Do you sleepwalk or something?" he asked, not even certain if he was joking.

She winced as she shifted to a sitting position, must have been lying there long enough to have her limbs go stiff.

"I was waiting for Tessa to get back to me."

"About what?"

She arched her back in a stretch, spreading her arms out. Clint had to look away from the scene of her long, graceful neck and the tempting curves under her tank top.

"Tessa had company when I walked in. She said she would call me when they were...you know, finished."

"I see." He glanced down at his watch. "It's past midnight. Way past."

"Guess she forgot."

More likely, they weren't yet "finished." "Do you want to try calling her?"

Nodding, she pulled her cell out of her pocket and dialed. Several beats passed then Clint heard Tessa's voice through the tiny speaker saying she couldn't answer.

"Straight to voice mail." Rita tossed her phone on the coffee table in front of them. "Guess I'll be enjoying the open-air lounge for a while longer."

"Why don't you just go back to your room. Tell them they've had enough time."

Her eyes grew wide. "No way. That was embarrassing enough the first time."

"Embarrassing how?"

"I sort of walked in on them."

Clint slapped a hand to his mouth, but not before he could stifle the burst of laughter.

Rita narrowed her eyes on him; her lips formed a tight line. "Ha ha. I'm glad you think that's funny."

"I'm sorry. It is pretty funny, knowing what I know of you." No doubt in the world Rita had turned redder than the woman who'd actually been caught in flagrante.

"What's that supposed to mean?"

"Never mind. It's not important."

"I think you might have just implied I'm a prude."

"If the shoe fits…yada yada."

She glared at him. "I'm going to choose to ignore that by changing the subject. How's Lizzie? Have you heard anything?"

Quite a deft way to change the subject, at that. Thankfully, there was at least some good news on that front. "I called her a little while after we returned. Looks like she and Jonathon went to dinner together. Crisis averted apparently."

"Thank goodness."

"Now for your crisis." He motioned to her and then around to the couches.

"I'd hardly consider this a crisis. I can always go ask for another room."

"Are you kidding? This place is continually booked. We had to reserve our rooms months ago."

Her shoulders sagged with defeat. Turning behind her, she punched the seat cushion and leaned back against it. "Looks like I'll have to make myself comfortable here awhile longer."

Like he would allow that to happen in a thousand years. Standing, he offered her his arm. "That's silly. Come with me."

She blinked up at him. He felt a resounding sense of relief when she finally stood up and took his hand. "Where to?"

"Just follow me." He knew she wasn't going to go along with his idea easily, but they could argue along the way.

"Where are we going? I'd like to know," she insisted even as she trailed behind him.

"I'm not going to let you sleep here all night. Not when there's a perfectly good suite we can share."

If she was counting, she would have to acknowledge all the times that Clint had come through for her in the few short days since he'd walked into that airport executive lounge. A nagging voice repeated in her head that none of it boded very well for her newly avowed goal to live more independently, reliant on her own devices.

Clint must have sensed her hesitation.

"It's a two-room suite. One bedroom and one living room complete with a long sofa and a connected door that can be closed."

"I'm not so sure that's a good idea."

"You'll have all the privacy you need."

Rita inhaled deeply as she contemplated his words. It made total sense. Definitely more sense than trying to get any sleep out here in an open lounge area. And frankly, she was exhausted between all the activity of the past few days and her sleepless night. Not to mention, she didn't want to be out here alone in case there were any visitors. Especially incorporeal ones like from the night before.

"It has been a rather long day." Two days, in fact. "And I would kill to wash my face and brush my teeth." Two routine tasks she'd really rather not wait until morning for.

"We can pick up some sundries from the night manager. I'll even let you have the bed."

She shook her head. "No way. If I do this, I insist on sleeping on the couch."

"Suit yourself."

"I haven't actually agreed."

Despite her words, he must have sensed her capitulation, as Clint further pleaded his case. "We have an all-day snorkeling adventure tomorrow. You'll need to be rested up."

Rita rubbed at her forehead, trying to release some of the tension that had suddenly gathered there and knotted itself under her scalp. She had no good reason to say no. And she was so bone tired. Her only options were to sleep out here, kick a sleeping man out of a warm bed that he was sharing with a warm body. Or she could take Clint up on his offer. Maybe she was too exhausted to think straight, because only one of those options seemed to make sense at the moment. Besides, they were both adults. Technically, she'd known him for years. They'd just spent the whole day together. Quite an enjoyable day, in fact. Well, except for the awkwardness toward the end that came after that soul-shattering kiss.

And that was it right there. She'd be following him to his room right this very minute ready to fall fast asleep, if it wasn't for that blasted kiss. Could she really be that close to him, practically in the same room, all the while knowing what it felt like to be held by him? The way he'd tasted. Her skin tingled as she recalled the way his hands had gripped her around the waist, held her tight up against him.

"Rita. Come on. Show some compassion."

"Compassion?"

"Do it for me. I will get absolutely zero sleep knowing you're out here by yourself. Plus, I think there's some heavy rain due later tonight."

"I'm pretty sure you just made that up. About the rain."

"I might have." He gave her a small smile. "You have to know you can trust me," Clint added, throwing down the proverbial gauntlet and making it almost impossible to say no.

She did trust him. Without any qualms or hesitation. She just wasn't so sure how much she trusted herself.

The man looked like sin. Rita adjusted the waistband of her swimsuit and tried to avert her gaze from where Clint stood on the deck of the boat. Beyond him the water of the Pacific Ocean gleamed like a sea of blue-green emeralds under the bright, shining mandarin-orange sun.

He'd been right about last night. Despite her

heightened awareness of him in the next room, her tiredness had won out in the end and she'd fallen asleep as soon as she'd collapsed on his couch. Hadn't even heard him when he'd come to throw the extra blanket over her. He'd also let her oversleep, so her run to the room to get her tankini for this snorkeling jaunt had been frantic and rushed.

Despite the unexpected lie-in, Rita felt like she could use several more hours of sleep.

No doubt, a set of puffy dark circles framed her bloodshot eyes. Well, it hardly mattered— her face would be under a mask, then submerged in water most of the day. Clint, by contrast, appeared awake and alert. He stood against the railing, bouncing on his heels to the rhythmic reggae music the captain had playing. A jovial crew ran around them, prepping for the first snorkeling stop.

For two people who had spent the night in the same suite, they were doing an impressive job of avoiding talking to each other.

The truth was, she'd been the one avoiding him. But it was for her own self-preservation. Every time she glanced at his face, her gaze fell to his lips and triggered a tingling sensation in hers.

Dreams of their kiss yesterday had haunted slumber all night. Images of her locked in his embrace framed against a backdrop of glimmering blue water and sparkling pink sand.

Stop it.

Well, she couldn't keep up the avoidance for long. The wedding wasn't for two more days still. Their paths were sure to cross at some point.

Bending down to reach for her mask, she came face-to-face with a set of sparkling blue eyes when she straightened.

"Hi, Tessa."

"Oh, my God, Rita. I'm so sorry I didn't text you last night. We fell asleep. We were just so tired."

"I kind of figured."

"I'm guessing you found a place to crash." She gestured to where Clint still stood, his tanned muscular back to them.

"Yes, I did," Rita simply replied. There would be no use in trying to correct Tessa's misguided insinuation. Nothing had actually happened between her and Clint overnight. Only in her dreams.

Tessa clapped her hands in front of her chest. "I figured you might." The woman was just too giddy this time of the day. She gave her a sly wink. "So it won't be a problem if Rob and I have the room to ourselves again tonight?"

Was she serious?

"I'm not so sure—"

Tessa's face fell, the smile dropping from her lips. She looked like a wounded puppy. Rita felt her jaw clench as she inwardly cursed. She had no reason to feel guilty. It was her room too.

"What about Rob's room? Perhaps you two can take turns," she offered.

Tessa pursed her lips. "His roommate apparently picked up the perky, smiley waitress at the cabana down the beach. Already told Rob he called dibs on the room."

What in the world? How was everyone in the wedding party so great at hooking up? And here she was, a fluttering, quivering mess just because Clint had kissed her on the beach. In fairness however, she'd never been kissed that way before. And it would probably never happen again. That notion had her heart sinking. Her eyes automatically found him once more. Her breath caught in her throat.

Tessa looked from one of them to the other. "I don't understand. I mean, clearly you two are—"

Rita cut her off. "We're not. Really, we're just friends."

Tessa didn't bother to hide her eye roll. "You could have fooled me. The way you two keep looking at each other."

Rita felt her cheeks flame with heat. Was she that obvious? Could the whole world tell that she was attracted like crazy to the bride's brother? How utterly horrifying.

"I'm sorry for assuming," Tessa continued. "I'll tell Rob he's out of luck tonight. Though I don't know where the poor guy is going to crash if his roommate brings the waitress there with him again."

There was a lounge area on the ground floor that wasn't terribly comfortable but could be considered an option, she almost told her. Rita sighed. It was like a domino effect. She felt herself capitulating. It wasn't like she didn't have a place to stay. Clint's suite did have ample room. And once she shut the door, it was like they weren't even sharing a space.

She studied Tessa's face. Her expression held more than disappointment. Much more. Rita got the feeling she was witnessing more than an island fling.

"You're falling for him, aren't you?"

To her utter surprise, the other woman's eyes started glistening with tears. "I've never felt this way before about anyone. He's gentle and sweet. And he makes me laugh. I can't bear to think about what's going to happen when we leave here. He lives on the opposite coast after all."

Rita took the other woman's hand in her own. "Oh, Tessa. I'm sure you two will figure something out."

"Do you really think so?" Hope shone through her eyes.

"I really do."

"Thanks." She sniffled. "I really hope we can."

"I'll be rooting for you." That comment earned her a wide smile.

Rita sighed with resignation. In the meantime, she could let them have these few remaining nights together. At least one of them had found their chance at happiness and love. Who was she to stand in the way? Tessa started to stand but she stopped her. "Consider the room all yours."

Clint couldn't really keep up with what Rita was trying to tell him. Something about the waitress from the poolside cabana bar and Tessa living on the opposite coast. And also something about Rob What's-His-Name who was one of the groomsmen and how much Tessa liked him.

In Clint's defense, it was hard to concentrate on her words when the sun was shining on her hair and making it glisten like liquid black silk. Her cheeks were touched by just enough tan that they'd turned an intriguing rosy color he'd be hard-pressed to describe. And don't even get him started on the bathing suit she was wearing. Modest by most standards, it showed just enough of her midriff to scream temptation. The rich scarlet color of the fabric complimented her skin tone in a way that had him losing his train of thought.

A thin gold chain around her ankle made him want to reach down and run his fingers over the charms she wore on it. Then he'd work his way slowly up her calves. Then higher.

He gave his head a shake.

He had to pay attention. She was trying to tell him something important. But all he could focus on was the fact that it appeared she would be staying with him again tonight. That's all he really needed to hear.

They were disembarking off the catamaran after a full day of snorkeling. All in all, not a bad way to spend several hours off the sunny coast of Hawaii. Only it didn't compare to the pleasant enjoyment of yesterday, when he'd had Rita to himself.

"So I guess I'll just come by after dinner some-time. As soon as Rob shows up. You don't mind, do you? I feel kind of awkward asking."

"It's no trouble at all, Rita."

She still looked apprehensive and stopped him as they walked along the beach back to the resort. "Please don't read anything into this."

Something sparked in his chest. After all the experiences they'd shared together so far on this trip, all the ways he'd opened up to her and vice versa, she felt the need to warn him about mak-ing assumptions. The notion stung more than he cared to admit.

"Why would I? I'd like to think you're not the type to be coy when it comes to asking directly for what you want from a man."

Her gasp of surprise told him his comment had hit home. Good, he'd meant for it to.

"Maybe this isn't such a great idea after all." Her voice held a plethora of doubt.

What did she expect? Was he also not supposed to read anything into the way she'd reacted to his touch? Or the way she'd moaned softly into his lips as he'd kissed her?

He didn't get a chance to respond as Lizzie stormed past them followed by Jonathon hot on her heels. Lizzie's anger was palpable, the steam rising from her almost a tangible sight.

Not again.

"Huh." Rita spoke behind him. "We returned the rock and everything."

Clint resisted the urge to go after them both and tell them to get it together already, that the attendees didn't have time for this childish behavior from the bride and groom. But he had his own ire to contend with.

"What do you mean exactly?"

She blinked up in surprise. "Clearly Lizzie and Jonathon are fighting again."

"I know that. What do you mean about me not reading into things when it comes to you?"

Rita stomped past him without answering, her footsteps splashing water onto his legs. Well, he wasn't about to let her get away. Catching up to her, he gently but firmly took her by the elbow.

"Care to answer?"

"I don't think I do. Forget about me staying in your suite tonight. Forget I even mentioned it."

"It's a little too late for that, don't you think? You've already told Tessa she could have the room."

She pulled her arm free. "I'll think of something."

Clint rubbed a hand down his face with frustration. "What is it with you?"

"I don't know what you mean."

"It means I noticed how you've been avoiding me the whole day. Barely spoke two words to me even though we've been on the same boat for the past several hours."

"I was enjoying the scenery."

"Sure, you were. You practically pulled a muscle trying to get sunscreen lotion on your back by yourself."

Her jaw dropped. "Are you actually saying you're upset because you wanted to rub lotion on my back and I didn't ask?"

Well, when she put it that way...

He ignored that and continued, "Then as we're disembarking, you finally remember my name and ask about staying in my suite. Only I better not get any high hopes that it might mean something."

"I'm sorry."

"And another thing—wait… What did you say?"

"I apologize. I shouldn't have ignored you. It's just hard to know what to say to you now."

Because he'd kissed her. She was clearly conflicted about it.

Well, so was he. But he refused to regret that it happened and very much hoped she didn't regret it either.

"This is all taking me a bit by surprise." She said it so softly, with such a wistful sadness in her voice. There was no denying the truth in her statement. He suddenly felt like a heel for the way he'd just behaved, making her feel the need to apologize to him.

"Yeah, I know. Apology accepted. And I'd love to have you as a suite mate again."

She finally smiled. "Maybe we can make a whole event of it. Rent a movie and do each other's hair. Like a real sleepover."

As far as jokes went, it was a pretty lame one. But Clint appreciated the attempt to lighten the mood.

He wasn't going to tell her just how impossible it had been to sleep last night, knowing she was only a few feet away. This thing between them, whatever it was, had him spinning and twisting about inside. He'd never felt anything like it.

How in the world was he supposed to ignore that for the next several days until they both went back to their regular, daily lives? He had no doubt Rita was just as bothered as he was. That kiss yesterday in the cave proved it. He wanted to make the most of the time they had here together still. In a way that wasn't awkward or strained.

He watched the remaining members of the wedding party as they slowly strolled past, some holding hands. Tessa and Rob were particularly engrossed in each other as they made their way along the beach. Rita sighed as they walked by.

"You were right yesterday, about everyone coupling up on this trip," Rita stated, echoing his thoughts. "It's not just my roommate and her groomsman."

Without allowing himself to think, he crooked a finger under her chin and lifted her face to look up at him. "Maybe we should too."

He'd shocked her. She visibly retreated as he said the words. "Oh, Clint. You have to understand. The timing is just so wrong."

Didn't she see that was his whole point? "It doesn't have to be, Rita. We have four more days on this island. We can make the most of it." Boldly, he stepped closer to her. "I know I want to kiss you again. I want to feel what I felt in that cave when you were in my arms. As often as I can before we have to bid our goodbyes once this is over."

The struggle behind her eyes was clear and tangible.

"Think about it." He dropped his hand. "In the meantime, my couch is yours tonight if you need it."

They were both silent as they slowly made their way back to the hotel lobby. Rita dared a glance at Clint's profile. The sleek, stylish sunglasses he had on made it difficult to gauge his expression. Dear Lord, he'd essentially just asked her to consider a mindless fling. He'd just thrown it out there, as if it was the most trivial thing in the world. Like asking her what she wanted to do for lunch later.

To his credit, he was being brutally honest. A heaviness settled into her chest. He wanted nothing more than a light, swift affair. His exact words were *before we have to bid our goodbyes*.

She'd be foolish to read anything more into his proposal.

Did she have the nerve to take him up on it? For just the next few days, could she really put aside her concerns and reservations and just enjoy herself? Live in this fantasy she found herself in?

Think about it, he'd said. As if she'd be able to think about anything else.

CHAPTER NINE

As FAR AS finally getting some sleep, tonight was no different than the previous two.

Clint threw his arm over his head and muttered a curse in the dark. Funny, he'd never been plagued by such relentless insomnia before this trip. Then again, never before had he ever had a woman so close yet so out of his reach.

The timing is just so wrong. The words Rita had spoken to him on the beach echoed through his head.

He grunted out loud. With thoughts like that floating through his mind, it was no wonder he couldn't sleep. A slight movement outside the glass door of the patio suddenly drew his attention. Apparently, he wasn't the only one who couldn't sleep. After crawling out of bed, he tugged the sheer curtain aside to see Rita standing by the railing, staring up at the moonlit sky. He opened the door slowly so as not to startle her.

"Decided to do some stargazing?"

She smiled at him as he walked closer to stand by her side. "It's very pretty. The sky is so clear, the moon so bright."

"Mmm-hmm."

"Why are you up?"

He shrugged. "Couldn't sleep."

"I hope I wasn't making too much noise out here." She reached up, started rubbing the back of her neck.

"You didn't wake me. Stiff?"

She rolled her head back and forth, working out some sort of kink. "No, it's not that."

"You didn't hurt yourself snorkeling, did you?"

He heard her laugh. "Only when I scraped by knee against the rough coral when I foolishly dived under and got too close. Just really wanted a better look."

That didn't explain what was wrong with her neck. Then he realized. "It's the couch. You can't be very comfortable on that thing."

"It's fine, Clint. I just fell asleep at an odd angle. It'll be all right once I knead out the knot at the base of my neck."

"Here." Without giving her a chance to protest, he reached over and started to massage the spot she'd been working. "Better?"

She sighed with satisfaction and Clint felt his mouth grow dry. For heaven's sake, he had to stop reacting to this woman's every movement. What in the world was wrong with him?

"Much better. In fact, I'm gonna go lie down again. Good night," she said with a small wave.

"Rita, wait."

She turned on her heel. "Yes."

Clearing his throat, he decided to just blurt it out. "The bed is huge. Too big for one person. Even with someone my size in it."

"Clint. I'm not sure it's wise for us to share a bed."

The proposal he'd made to her earlier on the beach sat like a proverbial elephant in the room. Maybe he should have never done it. What had he been thinking? Rita wasn't the type to have a meaningless fling. She deserved more from a man than what he'd offered her.

"Listen, if you're concerned that I'll take your sleeping in the bed as some sort of answer to what I proposed earlier, you don't have to worry about that."

"But you did propose it, Clint."

"And now it's totally in your hands. Whatever

you decide, whenever you decide it. The ball is completely in your court."

She chewed her bottom lip. "We'll only be sharing the bed in the interest of comfort and practicality?"

He nodded. "I honestly don't see why we can't. I'd offer to take the couch myself if I thought for one instant that you'd allow it." But that was not the way she was wired.

Rita was the type of woman who tried to sleep in a lobby lounge chair so her roommate could have some privacy. She was the type to make sure a wandering dog wasn't a stray and that it made it back to its home safely. She was the kind of woman any man would be proud to have in his life.

Any man who deserved her. And he certainly didn't qualify. She warranted more than he'd ever be willing or able to give. And if that didn't make him selfish for the way he'd casually asked her for a fling, he didn't know what would.

"If it makes you feel better, I can't seem to fall asleep anyway," he told her. "I fully intended to power up the laptop and try to get some work done."

"All night?"

"I've done it before." More often than he could count, particularly those early days when he was getting his business off the ground as well as working ten-hour shifts to lend a hand at the various construction sites.

She glanced behind him into the room. "It does appear rather large."

"A California king they called it when they sold me the package. It would be a shame to let it go to waste."

"Are you sure I'm not kicking you out of your bed?"

She remained where she stood.

"You're not," he offered in as reassuring a tone as he could muster.

"All right, then. I could use the rest."

He stepped over to the door and held it open for her, trying to ignore the enticing citrus-and-coconut smell of her skin as she walked past.

The chances of him actually getting any work done were almost zero.

She could hear him breathing deeply in the other room. He'd set up his laptop and gotten to work, all right. But then he'd promptly fallen asleep. She could tell by the steady rhythm of his breath.

On the same uncomfortable couch he'd rescued her from.

How was she supposed to relax knowing he was out there and she was in here on a nice comfortable mattress?

Sighing, she lifted away the covers and walked over to the other room.

Yep, out cold. Clint was sprawled on the couch with his legs and arms dangling off the ends. It was way too small for him. His head was bent on the back cushion at the same odd angle she'd woken up in earlier. As it was, she'd barely avoided a nasty tension headache due to the awkward position. She didn't want the same for Clint, especially considering it would be her fault.

She gave him a gentle nudge on the arm and quietly called his name.

He opened his eyes almost immediately. It took a few blinks but eventually she watched as he focused on her face. "What's wrong? Are you all right? Your neck hurt again?"

An odd sensation stirred in the pit of her stomach. His first reaction upon wakening had been concern for her. How many people in her life could she say that about? Only her mother came to mind. When she wasn't soundly disappointed in her. Which was all too often.

"I'm fine," she responded, touched even further when he blew out a relieved breath. "But I think we should make this a true slumber party."

He sat up and rubbed his eyes. "Huh?"

"We can share the bed. Like a real sleepover. What do you say?"

With a groggy smile, he got up and followed her to the bed.

"Thanks," Clint whispered once they'd both crawled under the covers. She could smell the subtle scent of his aftershave even though it was now hours old. She'd taken a whiff of the bottle in the bathroom earlier, recognized the scent now.

"Please don't thank me for letting you sleep in your own bed, Clint. It makes me feel quite guilty."

"Sorry."

Now he was apologizing; that was somehow even worse. "Good night."

"Good night, sweet Rita."

The endearment evoked a small spark of pleasure in her chest. Would he have ever spoken that way if he wasn't half-asleep? Doubtful. "Get some sleep."

She heard him yawn beside her then turn to his side. Eventually, his breathing seemed to return to the same steady rhythm she'd heard earlier when he'd been asleep. So it surprised her when he spoke again a few moments later. Even more shocking were his words.

"Did you love him, Rita? You must have loved him deeply if you married him, right?"

Clint realized with a start that he'd actually voiced the question out loud. Damn his sleep-fogged brain and the tongue it had set loose. Rita's gasp of surprise left no doubt that she was now stunned and uncomfortable. Probably regretted inviting him into the bed for their "sleepover" as she called it.

They were both wide-awake now.

"That's quite the question."

"I'm sorry," he replied, with genuine regret. It wasn't like he actually wanted to know the answer. "It's none of my business."

"I married him. We both took vows to love and cherish each other."

Her words felt like individual blows to his gut. He'd been right; he hadn't really wanted to know. To top it off, Rita's tone held a strange tightness.

He'd insulted her. After all, his question insinuated she may have married a man she wasn't in love with.

Clint wished he'd never even opened the can of worms. "I'm sorry it didn't work out," he lied.

The truth was, he wasn't sorry one bit that she was here solo. This trip would have been a far less memorable experience sans the time they'd spent together. He supposed that made him selfish, considering he had no claim to her. He'd probably only see her in passing, if ever, once they left this island.

"Jay and I grew up as childhood friends. In a way, we've always loved each other."

The blows kept coming. The tightening in his gut had him cringing. He had to acknowledge it as jealousy. As if he had the right.

"But it wasn't the type of love that should have led to marriage."

That threw him for a loop. Was she implying they were just friends? If so, why would they have tied the knot? There didn't seem to be any kind of financial reason, and she didn't seem the type of woman who would let something like a financial concern influence any kind of decision. Let alone a commitment like marriage. He knew about her father's cultural roots. Had that had something to do with it?

The questions hammered through his brain. As much as he wanted the answers, he resisted asking. She would share if she was ready. He'd done enough prying.

Enough time went by that he figured she wasn't ready. But then she surprised him by turning to face him. Her hands cupped under her cheek, the intensity in her eyes shone even through the darkened night.

"Someone like you wouldn't understand."

She was right about that. He didn't understand any of it. Nor could he explain his own reaction to it all. "I'd really like to."

"I didn't grow up the way most American girls do. In many ways, my family was very typical. In others, not so much."

So, it was cultural.

"My father didn't want to leave anything to chance when it came to his little girl, his only child."

"That actually sounds like pretty much any decent American dad."

He heard her inhale deeply. "Yes. And no." She

blew out a breath. "He could be confusing as a parent."

Outside the glass wall, the moon slowly faded behind a cloud, casting longer darker shadows through the room.

"How so?"

"Well, for one, he made sure to instill a fierce sense of independence and strength in me. Made sure I knew how capable I was."

That much was clear in her every action, every nuance.

"But by the same token, there were all these decisions he'd made himself that he just wanted me to accept."

"Like marrying the man he'd chosen for you."

"Yes."

"What else?"

"My choice of vocation. He really grappled with the fact that I wanted to spend my life taking care of animals."

"Where was your mother in all this? Did she have any opinions?"

"My mom grew up in the Midwest. A rancher's daughter with five older brothers. Let's just say she made it a life goal to be a dutiful wife.

A quality she seemed shocked that I didn't inherit from her."

"Wow. That is shocking."

"What? That I'm so different from my mother?"

"That you have five uncles," he joked, hoping it would lend a little levity to such a serious conversation. To his surprise, the remark earned him a small laugh.

"Yeah, I have like a million cousins. Holidays are fun."

"I guess my holidays will be different going forward too. Now that Lizzie's getting married. Jonathon's also got a large family." Clint only now realized the notion had been on his mind for a while, he'd just never brought it out into the forefront until now. His life was about to change almost as much as his sister's.

"You're going to make a great uncle yourself someday."

He groaned and rubbed a hand over his face. "Not anytime soon, I hope. I need some time to prep my embarrassing uncle game."

Her laugh echoed like a song through the darkness. "Why do I get the feeling you're more likely to be the uncle who shows up with armloads of gifts, spoils the kids rotten, then leaves a ridiculous mess for the parents to clean up after he's left?"

"I shall aspire to such greatness." Clint chuckled. The humor was short-lived.

"Sorry to say, my next family gathering will be as awkward and trying as the last one," Rita said, her voice so low it was barely a soft whisper.

"How come?"

"My father has barely said more than a few words to me since the divorce."

"He's angry?"

"No. Worse. He's disappointed." Maybe he'd imagined it, but he thought she might have wiped at her cheek. The thought of her crying made him wince inside.

"He's convinced I made a foolish decision in ending my marriage. That Jay and I were meant for each other and I blew it. For no discernible reason as far as he's concerned."

"Maybe you should explain your reasons then."

Her response was a long sigh. "My father isn't an easy man to talk to. I'm not sure exactly what I would say."

"I think it will come to you."

"You think so, huh?"

"I do. You still have a chance to try."

She shifted ever so slightly. "You're thinking of your own parents, aren't you?"

"I guess I am. My folks were gone often but when they were around, it was a completely different dynamic."

"In what way?"

"The world just felt whole, complete. Then suddenly it wasn't. And I had to accept the fact that life would never feel that way again."

"You were so strong, Clint."

Touching as it was, he chose to ignore her praise. He'd had no choice but to act strong. "Perhaps your dad just needs a nudge. If he's the man you've described so far, he'll come around."

"I hope so." She shifted closer to him; he could feel her sweet breath against his chin. "I've never discussed any of this with anybody before. I want you to know that."

Clint couldn't help reaching for her. He ran a gentle knuckle down her cheek, then down lower to her long graceful neck, felt her swallow under the tip of his finger. Electricity shot through his arm straight down to his feet. "I don't know if you and your ex belonged together or not. But I can't imagine being the man who had to let you go."

Her only response was a sharp intake of breath. Clint wanted desperately to pull her to him, to rub the tension in her shoulders, tension so palpable he could see it despite the dark. He clenched his fists; he wouldn't touch her. It would be wrong to do so. She'd confided in him just now. He wouldn't betray that confidence by giving in to the desire he'd felt for her since they'd first laid eyes on each other.

His subconscious must have had other plans.

When they woke up the next morning, she was in his arms, head nuzzled against his neck. Her hair fanned like a dark silk scarf around his chest and shoulders. He didn't move a muscle for fear of waking her.

Unwilling to let her go just yet.

CHAPTER TEN

RITA SEEMED TO LIKE her showers extremely hot, judging by the steam wafting out from the bottom of the bathroom door. He tried not to imagine her behind that door, inside the shower stall, her smooth bare skin under the hot water. Was she lathering up right now, running a bar of soap over her curves?

Oh, man, he had it pretty bad.

He had to step away, before he gave in to the urge to knock and ask if she wanted company. Grabbing the pot of coffee he'd ordered earlier from room service, he poured a cup and walked onto the balcony to take in the early-morning weather. Another gorgeous day it looked like. Was there anything on the schedule wedding related? He couldn't even keep track anymore. Plus, he'd been a little distracted. In the distance, the ocean waves crashed gently along the sand of the beach. The vacant mountain was partially covered in fog, the top quarter not even visible.

The shrill sound of his cell phone in his pocket interrupted his thoughts. He pulled it out and clicked without looking at the screen. Most likely, it was Lizzie calling to give him an update. He'd left her several voice mail messages to check on her yesterday.

He was wrong. A husky, rich feminine voice greeted him when he answered.

"Did I wake you?" Maxine asked with her usual purr.

An urge to disconnect and pretend the call was dropped entered his mind. But he immediately nixed that idea. As much as he wanted to avoid this conversation, running was not his style.

"No. I've been up for a while."

She hesitated before speaking again, perhaps sensing the lack of enthusiasm in his voice. "How are things down there?"

"Fine. Everything's fine."

"And our bride? How's Lizzie faring?"

Our? Clint didn't miss the subtle meaning behind the use of the word. So now Lizzie was somehow her relation, as well. He rubbed his forehead. There was no doubt why she'd called and where this phone call was headed. Not that he'd had any doubt to begin with.

A pang of regret settled in his gut. Maxine wasn't a bad person. She really wasn't. But this thing between them had run its course.

"I've had a nightmare of a week," she told him.

Ah, so that explained the sudden call. Maxine needed a sounding board for the latest professional rejection. And someone to tell her how great she was, that whoever had turned her down was a bumbling fool of an idiot to do so.

He just didn't have the patience right now. "I'm sorry to hear that, Maxie. Hope it gets better for you."

He could almost feel her surprise bounce off the satellite and into the small speaker. "That's all you have to say? Don't you want to hear what happened? It was just awful, Clint."

He didn't have to respond. She continued without giving him a chance to, "The studio said they loved me when I went in and read. But I never even got a call back. Turns out, they've decided to go with that new Australian model who wants to break into the US movie market. I can't even believe they'd make that decision…"

Clint lost focus as she went on. Not that he didn't feel bad for her, he really did. But this was a pattern for her. A complete immersion in melancholy until the next gig came along. She had beauty, talent and connections. The next one always came along. Which is what he would have normally told her back in the United States.

Today, he didn't have the will for it. Nor the desire.

"Sorry, Maxie. You're a talented actress."

"Do you really think so?"

"I do."

He heard her sigh across the line. "You're so good for me, Clint." She paused for several beats. "I miss you."

There it was. He couldn't bring himself to answer, to lie to her. So he did the best he could. "Thank you."

Her gasp of outrage was unmistakable. "Thank you? That's what you're going to say to me?" Her question came through like the demand that it was. Demand that he apologize and thank his lucky stars that she'd deemed him worthy of the contact and this phone call.

Hard to believe a few short days ago he would have gone along, would have played the little game. Now he couldn't believe he'd ever had the patience for it.

"Sorry, Maxie," he repeated, more than ready to have this call over with.

"I accept your apology," she said with a breathless huff. "Now, I have great news for you."

"What's that?"

"I've decided I have to see you. Soon. I'm having my assistant arrange a flight right now."

Damn it. He should have seen that coming. The water shut off in the bathroom and he heard the shower stall click open. An immediate image of Rita dripping wet and naked flashed in his mind and he had to lean over the balcony railing to keep from doubling over.

Whatever Maxine was saying was a stream of static; he couldn't even focus on her words. "Max, I don't think that's a good idea. I think we both need to move on. Individually."

"I don't understand."

Oh, honey. Sighing, he tried to wrangle his calmest, most soothing voice. "I think you do."

After listening to a stream of curse words and several insults hinting at his questionable heritage, Clint finally figured Maxine was spent for now. He told her goodbye as gently as he could and clicked off the call.

Up until a few days ago, he'd sworn all he'd

ever want from a relationship was some idle companionship and a little fun. He couldn't be so certain of that conviction now. He'd shared parts of himself with Rita that he'd never opened up to anyone else. Her face was the first thing he pictured upon wakening in the morning. And the last image he had before falling asleep at night. He heard her laughter in his head and couldn't stop thinking about her when they weren't together.

Now, watching Rita as she stepped out of the bathroom with a thick terry-cloth towel wrapped around her middle and her glorious hair piled high atop her head, a wave of doubt made him wonder. About his feelings for Rita. About what he'd proposed to her on the beach after snorkeling, essentially a short-term, casual relationship for the duration of this trip. Up until now, he'd been all about such casual and meaningless relationships.

When it came to Rita, was that really enough? Or did he in fact want more?

Clint tried for the umpteenth time to focus on the column of figures his administrative assistant had emailed that morning. Rita had gone ahead to breakfast. Having been woefully negligent in answering any business emails, Clint regretfully told her he'd meet her there after responding to the more urgent messages.

A knock on the door waylaid his next attempt at concentration.

Must be the bellhop. He'd asked the front desk to bring all of Rita's stuff to his suite as soon as feasible. So she wouldn't have to keep returning to her room to retrieve various articles of clothing. It occurred to him before opening the door that he'd never actually gotten a chance to tell her about her things being moved. Well, it would be a pleasant surprise.

But the man standing across the threshold wasn't the bellhop. It was his future brother-in-law.

"Clint. We gotta talk, man."

Rita couldn't decide if the steam surrounding her was coming from the pot of hot water at the center of her table or directly out of her ears.

The man had some kind of nerve.

Clint hadn't made it down to join her yet. Which was probably not a good thing for him because the longer she sat here, the angrier she was getting. Finally, she watched him descend down the winding staircase and toward the dining area. He made a beeline when he saw her, his smile wide and cheery.

That wouldn't last.

"Hey, beautiful. Did you start without me?"

"Have a seat, Clint."

The smile faded. Pulling out a chair, he sat and folded his arms in front of him. "Something wrong?"

"As a matter of fact, there is."

"What's the matter? You look mad."

Wasn't he observant. She resisted the urge to sarcastically clap to congratulate him on it. "That's because I am."

"At me? Whatever for?"

He really had no idea. Well, she would explain then. "I went to my room before coming down for breakfast, wanting to drop off my nightclothes."

Understanding dawned in his eyes; his Adam's apple bobbed up and down as he swallowed. "And your stuff wasn't there."

"That's right. Tessa said a hotel employee had come in and asked her to gather everything that was mine. He'd been told to take it elsewhere. By you."

"Yes, I asked them to deliver it all to my suite."

"I caught the man in the hallway before he got to your door," Rita bit out, recalling how flustered the poor employee had been. Torn between following earlier directives or listening to the agitated woman telling him not to.

"I don't see the problem. I was simply trying to spare you from having to run back and forth every morning."

"That wasn't your decision. And it certainly wasn't one for you to make without even discussing it with me."

"It slipped my mind, okay? For what it's worth, it wasn't due to any kind of assumption about what I asked you yesterday."

The sudden further surge of anger had her gripping the table. "It absolutely better not have been."

"I just told you it wasn't. Why is this such a big deal?"

Did he really not see why? For heaven's sake, she'd gone to her room only to find all of her things gone. Without anyone telling her why.

Their server appeared right then, sparing him the reply Rita was about to deliver.

"What can I get for you both?"

Her appetite had evaporated but she needed something to calm the queasy waves in her stomach. "Just toast for me, thanks."

Clint ordered a meat-and-cheese omelet, then turned his attention back to her. "I'm sorry if I made an incorrect assumption," he told Rita after the woman had left. "I just figured you'd be staying with me the rest of the trip."

His words carried an intimacy they weren't quite ready for. She hadn't even given him an answer yet. More accurately, she knew *he* wasn't ready. That's why the whole fiasco with her possessions had her so wound up. He was making assumptions about the two of them, without any hint of awareness on his part. Evidently, he didn't see that.

"I simply would have appreciated some consultation before you went ahead and made decisions on my behalf."

"You are blowing this way out of proportion." His voice was hard, firm. He leaned over, rested his forearms on the table. For a moment, she felt a twinge of apprehension at the hardened glint in his eyes. Right now, he seemed irked, as well. Escalation was never a good thing.

But her point had to be made. She wasn't about to back down.

"They are my things. I decide where they stay. And nothing said I was going to spend another night in your room. I told Tessa we would make that call day to day."

"You don't want to stay in the room, just say so."

She flung her napkin on the table. "This has nothing to do with where I'm sleeping at night. That's not the point. Not at all."

"I guess I'm missing your point. Exactly what is it?"

How much clearer could she be? "Don't make decisions on my behalf. No one gave you such a right nor a claim."

His eyes grew wide. Without an answer, he pushed his chair back and stood to leave. "I've lost my appetite." Well, that made two of them.

"My door is open if you need tonight. Without any expectations whatsoever. Bring your things, don't bring them. Totally up to you."

Rita's jaw clenched with frustration. "That's my whole point."

He shook his head. "Whatever you decide, have a pleasant day."

Turning to leave, Clint only made it about one step from his chair. His sister ran down the stairs at that very moment and made her way to their table, her eyes blazing.

"Oh, no, you don't, big brother. You're not going anywhere." Lizzie pulled his chair back out. "Have a seat. We need to talk."

Okay. Rita glanced from one sibling to the other. This was something of a new, unexpected development. Looked like her own tiff with Clint was going to have to wait.

Things did not appear to be going his way this morning.

She started to get up. "I should probably give you two some privacy."

Lizzie held up a hand to stop her. "No, Rita. Please stay. I'd kind of like a third party here. It might keep me from causing too much of a scene."

Seemed a little late for that, but Rita figured she wouldn't voice that out loud.

Even given her displeasure with him at the moment, Rita shot Clint a questioning look. She wasn't going to stay if it made him uncomfortable. He gave her a small affirmative nod.

"What exactly did you say to my fiancé this morning?" Lizzie demanded of her brother.

"Hey, settle your tone there, sis."

"Just tell me what you said to him."

"He came down to talk to me. Maybe you should be having a conversation with him. Whatever it's about."

Rita found herself fascinated. An only child, she had no firsthand knowledge of sibling angst. Whatever Clint had said to Jonathon, it appeared Lizzie was ready to thrash him for it.

"Oh, I did talk to him," Lizzie said. "It seems he's working for you now."

"So?"

Lizzie slammed both hands on the table. The couple at the neighboring table gave them a startled glance. "So? Why would you offer my fiancé a job? First of all, he's an attorney. You own a construction firm. How blatantly obvious that it's nothing more than a nepotistic gesture."

"I consult with attorneys all the time."

"International law attorneys? You need one of those in-house, do you?"

"Look," Clint began, "he came to me to say he's been edgy and worried. It's why he's been snapping at you. Things aren't going well at work for him. He thinks his days at the law firm may be numbered."

"I know all that."

That seemed to take Clint aback. "You do?"

"Of course, I do. He's my fiancé. We actually share our fears and joys and concerns with each other."

"Then why did he come to see me?"

"Not to ask you for a job!"

"Then what?"

"Nothing. He wasn't asking you for anything. He simply wanted to explain to his fiancée's brother why he might be behaving on edge lately."

Clint squinted against the sun. "Huh."

"But somehow you offered him a job and I'm guessing you didn't take no for an answer."

"Hold on. That's not how it went down."

Lizzie's mouth tightened. "Right. Because you're never overbearing and assuming at all." Sarcasm dripped from her lips.

"If he didn't want the job, he could have just said so."

"Clint. He said he tried. But you just acted like you'd solved everything and showed him the door. Guess what, bro?"

"What?"

"He doesn't want to work for his brother-in-law. He wants to find his own way out of this."

Rita didn't miss the clear sense of pride in Lizzie's voice. Clint must have heard it too. It was hard to miss.

"But now he has all sorts of doubts. Thanks to you."

"What? Why?"

"Now he can't help but think maybe he should take your offer. Because how would he feel if nothing panned out for him and he'd turned you down?"

Clint shrugged, gave his sister a look like she was missing something terribly obvious. "Just tell him the offer stands whenever he wants it."

Wow. Rita wanted to grab his shoulders and give him a hard shake. Not only had he missed the point, it had blown right past him without even entering the strike zone. Lizzie visibly deflated in her chair.

"Oh, Clint," his sister began. "Don't you know what telling him that would do to him? How much worse it would make all this?"

Clint threw his hands up with exasperation. "Fine, go tell him the offer is rescinded. To forget I ever made it."

He really didn't get it, Rita thought. An unwelcome twinge of sympathy stirred in her heart. At this point, she couldn't tell if she felt worse for him or Lizzie. Or even Jonathon. Clint was somehow internally programed to solve any issue he came across. Whether people wanted solutions from him or not.

Lizzie slowly stood, every inch of her dripping resignation. "Enjoy your breakfast, big brother."

She gave Rita a small wave and turned on her heel to leave.

Clint watched her back for several moments before clearing his throat.

Rita scrambled for something to say. Anything. The words failed her. Lizzie was right; she knew that. But there was something so defeated in Clint as he'd watched his sister leave, Rita couldn't help but feel moved by it. Her earlier anger at him notwithstanding.

"You'll have to excuse me," he told her, then stood and walked away in the opposite direction. Away from his sister.

And away from her.

It took all his will not to punch a hole in the wall when Clint got back to his room. Was every female in his orbit put there just to vex him? He plopped himself down on the unmade bed and tried to clear the fog of confusion from his head. Just a few short hours ago, he was lying in this very spot with Rita's soft, supple body nestled against him.

Now he wasn't even sure if they were on speaking terms. And for what? Because he hadn't wanted her inconvenienced.

As for his sister, he couldn't even fathom that one. He really thought Jonathon had come to him looking for help with his next position. How was he supposed to know the man simply needed to vent?

Usually when people came to him directly it was absolutely because they needed something. And unlike Rita, when he did something he thought was considerate, usually they were thankful. Not ready to bite his head off like she'd clearly wanted to.

He needed to get out of here. Out of this room, away from this resort. Though the sun was already bright and hot and it was probably way too steamy for a run, he figured he needed it. Or he really would punch a wall.

Pulling on his running shoes, he made his

way out of the hotel and onto the beach. The next forty-five minutes was a grueling stretch of self-torture. Clint was near heaving for breath by the time he made it back. It was worth it. Every ounce of exertion had helped to vent his frustration and clear his head. He'd almost been able to eradicate the image of Rita shooting proverbial daggers at him this morning. Almost.

Despite his good intentions, she was rip-roaring mad at him. And so was his sister.

Clint rubbed the sweat off his forehand with the back of his arm and made his way to the elevator. He had to go see Lizzie. Then he had to clear things up with Jonathon. He couldn't have this hanging over their heads during the wedding. He'd do a mea culpa, even if he couldn't quite grasp exactly what his transgression was.

With reluctance but determination, he punched the floor Lizzie's room was on and knocked on her door moments later.

"Come in. It's not locked."

He wondered if she would be granting entry if she knew it was him. Opening the door, he hesitantly ducked his head in. "You sure I'm welcome?"

His sister sat at a vanity, her arms outstretched

in front of her. Several bowls of liquid sat in front of her along with a variety of brushes and colored pencils like he'd never seen before. Lizzie motioned for him to come inside. He did so and shut the door behind him.

Then stopped in his tracks when Rita suddenly walked out of the bathroom. What was she doing here? She carried a glass bowl with some type of reddish pudding concoction.

She quirked an eyebrow at him when she saw him.

"Am I interrupting something?" Clint asked. "You doing each other's nails?" Great, maybe they were bonding over their mutual disgust of all things Clint Fallon.

"Rita's giving me henna tattoos. A bridal design in honor of my wedding."

"A hen of *what*?"

Rita shot an exaggerated eye roll in his direction. "A henna. Tattoo."

As if that cleared it up. "Right."

"Here, I'll show you," Lizzie said and lifted her foot.

He drew closer to see an elaborate array of designs adorning her right ankle. It was a complicated design of swirls and patterns, drawn in some type of orange-reddish ink. He'd never seen anything like it.

"You did that?" he asked Rita, incredulous.

"She sure did," Lizzie answered. "She's going to do my hands next."

He was beyond impressed. Considering the skin on a human foot wasn't the smoothest, particularly around the ankle, the design showed a tremendous amount of detail and a very steady hand. Though, he shouldn't be surprised. After all, part of her profession was performing surgery on small animals. But the pattern on his sister's foot said she also had a striking amount of artistic skill.

"Wow." It was the only word he could summon.

"Amazing, isn't she?"

Yeah, she certainly was. Every time he turned around, she seemed to do something or say something that drove that point home. He studied her now as she sat down on the velvet seat of a short metal stool in front of his sister. She dipped one of the wooden sticks in the bowl of pudding and began to work on Lizzie's right hand.

"You're very sweaty." Rita finally addressed him, throwing the comment over her shoulder without looking at him.

"Yeah, I, uh, went for a run."

"Did it help?"

"Yes. It helped a lot. Which is why I'm here." Clint focused his gaze on his sister's face. "Look, the last thing I want is to have you upset with me as I'm walking you down the aisle."

Lizzie pursed her lips, as if she were holding back a sob. Damn it. He didn't need that. He could handle her anger way better than he could deal with her sadness. "I don't want that either, big brother."

"I'll clear the air with Jonathon. I'll find him later and buy him a beer. Or maybe one of those Hawaiian mai tais."

"The ones they bring out all aflame?"

He grinned, relieved that things seemed to be smoothing over. "Yeah. Those ones. Better yet, I'll make him buy me one."

"I think he'd like that, Clint."

"Good. Don't give the whole job thing another thought, all right?"

"It's a deal." She suddenly smiled wide and looked down to where Rita was painstakingly drawing on her hand. "Hey, I think Clint needs a henna tattoo also. What do you think?"

Uh-oh. What had he just walked into here? Rita stopped what she was doing.

"I suppose. It's not typically something men have done."

"My brother is far from typical. Have a seat," she ordered. "She'll do you as soon as she's finished with mine."

Turned out, that didn't take long. Lizzie jumped up when she was finished and admired the artwork. "I'm going to go find Jonathon and show him. Do Clint's now," she directed before leaving the room.

An awkward silence hung in the air when it was just the two of them. Clint blew out a breath. "I don't know. I've never had a henna tattoo before. Don't think I really want one now. But what the bride wants…"

"The bride gets," Rita finished for him. "Here." She motioned for him to sit.

"That looks really sharp," Clint commented on the wooden stick she'd picked up.

"Don't worry. I'm not planning on stabbing you with it. Though the thought has occurred to me."

"Um…thanks?"

"Let's just say it's a good thing you knew enough to make amends with Lizzie just now."

He tried not to react as her soft, warm fingers moved over his skin while she worked. Sweet heavens. How was he supposed to sit still and resist the temptation to turn around and yank her into his arms when she was touching him like this?

He tried to focus on the conversation. "At the risk of a stab, I'm going to admit that my apology was more to regain the peace than any kind of actual understanding about what I did that was so wrong."

Her fingers stilled. "You honestly don't know?"

"I thought I was helping, Rita."

Her voice was soft when she spoke again as she resumed slowly working on his back. "That's not what Jonathon came to you for. Nor what he needed."

"How was I supposed to know that?"

She leaned closer, her tempting breath hot against his ear. "Perhaps you could have listened."

"I thought I had. And what I heard was that he needed a more secure job. Why would I not offer that to him when I can?"

"Because it only served to make you feel better."

Harsh.

"You're used to taking over," Rita continued. "You're used to exerting control in order to
fix things. Whether the situation calls for it or
not. You did the same thing when you thought I
needed my things to be moved into your suite."

Why was that so wrong? "Yeah, well, I guess
I had to learn from a young age that someone
had to take the lead when things needed fixing.
My parents were gone and the grandmother in
charge of us could barely take care of herself."
He bit out a curse. The last thing he wanted was
to sound defensive. She wouldn't understand. For
all their faults, Rita had grown up with two very
involved parents—perhaps overly involved—who
made sure to give her stability and structure. He'd
done his best to do the same for his sister, for
better or worse. "Lizzie never fully appreciated
what it took to just survive back in those days."
Which was fine with him. It was bad enough that
one of them was terrified about the uncertainty
of their future. Lizzie was too busy grieving to
fully comprehend exactly how tenuous their reality had become. He'd had to be the one to plan
for their future, to make sure they'd be safe and
secure. Their grandmother certainly couldn't be
counted on. All the burden had fallen like a ton

of bricks securely on Clint's shoulders. No, he'd never talked to Lizzie back then about all the nights he'd lain awake, fighting off near-crippling anxiety. And Lord knew there wasn't anyone else to talk to.

Several beats passed before Rita answered, "Perhaps she would have understood, if you'd bothered to ever tell her."

He hadn't seen any point in that. "She had enough to contend with. I didn't want her bothered with anything more than she had to."

"Hmm. And despite that tendency of yours, Lizzie has still managed to turn into quite a competent and mature young lady."

Clint gave his head a shake. Despite? "What's that supposed to mean?"

She released a deep sigh and he could feel her warm breath against his shoulder and upper back. "It means that you were an incredibly competent guardian for your sister. Anyone can see that, Clint."

"But?"

"But people need room to grow and make their own mistakes. And often all they're looking for is some reassurance and emotional support."

He couldn't come up with a response to that.

Of course she had a point. But he didn't have many choices back then. He could only do what he thought was right. No one had been there to guide him after all. And what did any of it matter now anyway? All past history not worth revisiting.

It took about another half hour for her to finish, where she mostly worked in silence. Half an hour of divine torture and temptation. Her fingers deftly moving over his skin. The warm touch of her hands on his back.

Finally, she stood. "You're done."

"Thanks."

He stole a look in the mirror. His jaw dropped.

"Not what you were expecting?"

She'd drawn an elaborate rendering of...of all things...a butterfly. He groaned out loud. "Great. This will look wonderful on the beach. I'll feel so manly as I sport my fresh butterfly tattoo."

She had the audacity to giggle. "You'll get used to it. Maybe after a year or two."

A year! Or two!

"Whoa. Wait a minute. This is permanent?"

"I thought you knew."

Clint felt a moment of panic, then noticed the

smile tugging at the corners of her lips. She was a lousy actress. "Sorry, couldn't resist."

"Ha ha. Can we say we're even then?"

"Even?"

She had to know what he meant. He wanted to put the argument of the morning behind them as well as the whole conversation they'd just had. He wanted to go back to the moment they'd woken up with her embraced in his arms.

A soft sigh escaped her lips. "You're a tough man to stay angry at, Clint Fallon. Yes, I suppose we're even."

That was definitely her up there.

Clint squinted up into the sun at the top of the rock cliff on the edge of the resort property. The same rock cliff that the resort guests jumped off into the ocean. It had taken him several beats to make sure but that was definitely Rita climbing to the top. Apparently, today was the day she made the jump herself. He couldn't help but recall the afternoon three days ago when they'd held hands and launched themselves together into one of the Seven Sacred Pools.

Looked like she wanted to do this one alone.

He'd been looking for Jonathon, who was supposed to be out on the beach somewhere, soaking up some last rays of sun as a free man before he said his vows tomorrow. But Clint's eyes had inexplicably been drawn to the rock wall, as if he'd sensed her presence there. Now she was gracefully ambling closer to the top. All thoughts of Jonathon forgotten, Clint made his way closer to the wall. There was a line of people waiting on top of it to go before her. Hopefully, that would give him enough time to reach a spot where he could watch her jump from fairly close by. A ridiculous part of him wished she'd asked him to go with her, wished that he was up there right now waiting to take the plunge with her in the way they had that day at the Seven Sacred Pools.

Well, he'd take the next best thing. He'd surprise her by greeting her with a dry, ready towel when she swam out afterward. Taking a quick detour to a resort shack, he grabbed two beach towels. He reached the side of the beach wall just as the person in front of Rita jumped in.

Her turn. Even from this distance he could see her anticipation; excitement was visible in her stance and posture. Taking a step back, he watched as she held her arms in front of her in an arch above her head. In the next instant, she launched herself headfirst into the water. A clean dive that hardly made a splash. If he wasn't worried about looking foolish to the beachgoers around him, he would have actually clapped.

Nothing was going to stop him from giving her a round of applause when she came out. Which didn't seem to be anytime soon. Clint waited as several moments went by. He still didn't see anyone out there who could be Rita. Had she broken the surface further down and he'd missed her?

That didn't seem likely. He'd been watching carefully for her.

A worrisome spike of apprehension stabbed his heart. He knew she was a good swimmer but what was taking so long? Even jumpers who'd gone in after her were already out and swimming to shore.

Deep breaths. He had to get a grip here. She hadn't been under that long. And she'd proven herself more than comfortable in the water both during their snorkeling adventure and when they'd swum at various spots on the Road to Hana.

But the nagging sensation in his chest persisted. He had to do something. He'd never forgive himself if something had gone wrong with her jump and he was just standing here like a dolt.

The wall was rough and jagged. It had to be that way under the water too. Rita could have very well hit her head.

The idea of that possibility and the image it evoked made up his mind. Kicking his sandals off, he dropped the towels and made a mad rush toward the water. He swam several feet faster than he would have thought possible then dived under when he got closer to the diving spot.

No sign of her.

Clint's heart pounded in his chest. He'd waited too long. He should have jumped as soon as it had occurred to him that she might be hurt. Sucking in a deep breath he dived under once more. Salt water stung his eyes and burned his throat as he stayed under too long to keep searching.

This couldn't be happening to him twice in one lifetime. To lose his parents in a boating accident was more than tragic enough. Fate couldn't be so utterly, shatteringly cruel.

He had to break the surface again, needed another lungful of air. There was nothing for it. Panic set in his veins, his heart hammering from exertion and fear.

It seemed to take forever to kick back to the top. A familiar face met him when he finally got there.

"Hey, Clint." She flashed him a brilliant smile. "I thought that was you. Did you see me jump?"

The sudden surge of relief he felt was almost instantaneously replaced with a blazingly intense fury.

"What the hell were you thinking?" Without waiting for an answer, he swam back toward the beach.

She was fast on his heels when he got there. "What exactly is your problem?" she asked.

Clint grabbed one of the towels he'd dropped on the sand earlier and handed it to her. She grasped it none too gently out of his hand even as she uttered a begrudging thank-you.

Leaning down, he grabbed the second one for himself. It was covered in grainy sand now— thanks to the wind—and the chafing sensation as he tried to dry off only served to irritate his nerves even further.

"I asked you what your problem is," Rita repeated. "Is there a reason you came into the water to yell at me?"

"My problem is that I thought you might be

floating out to sea about to become a tasty morsel of shark food."

She stalled in the act of towel drying her hair. "What? Why in the world would you think that?"

"Because you didn't come up. Do you have any idea how long you were under?"

She gave a slight shrug. "I stayed under as long as I could."

"Whatever for?" To give him a heart attack perhaps?

Her jaw clenched. "I appreciate that you were worried. But you needn't keep yelling at me. As you can see, I'm perfectly fine. There was no reason for you to come after me. And no reason at all for the way you're behaving now."

Clint sucked in a breath trying to calm himself. It didn't work. She had no idea how much of a scare she'd just caused.

The thought of her hurt, struggling under the water had unnerved him unlike anything else he could recall.

She really had no clue.

"Why would you even do such a thing by yourself?" He realized people were starting to stare but he couldn't seem to lower his voice. The panic still pounded through his system.

"Not that I owe you an explanation. But I've been wanting to do that jump for days and there weren't that many people up there for once." She crossed her arms in front of her chest. "And frankly, I'm starting to feel a little resentful at your tone. It's really none of your business who I jump with, if anyone at all."

Resentful? None of his business?

That was it. Between her inflated reaction this morning to the moved luggage and the vitriol she was feeding him right now, he'd had it.

"You know what, Rita? I believe you're right." He picked up his shirt and sandals. "Feel free to spend the night in the suite if you want. Or not. It's up to you. If not, I guess I'll see you at the wedding."

He didn't give her a chance to respond.

Of all the...

Rita watched Clint's retreating back as he stomped away down the beach. All she'd wanted to do was take a refreshing plunge into the water. Then, as she was under, a glorious sea turtle had swum by, so close she could have reached out and touched it. A truly magnificent, breathtaking beauty of a creature she didn't want to stop admiring. So she'd stayed down there as long as she could. Until her lungs had started to squeeze in her chest and her cells had begun to cry out in protest for oxygen.

Okay, so maybe it had been a little long. But if Clint had just taken the time to listen, she could have explained all that. She might have even asked him to go back in with her so that they could look for it together. Maybe she would have confided that he was the first person she thought of sharing the experience with, had even felt a pang of longing to have him there with her. He hadn't even given her a chance to speak.

Instead, he'd chosen to stand on a public beach, in front of countless people, and loudly chastise her.

In fact, it had been his first reaction. To be domineering and overbearing, two traits she'd had more than her fair share of in her life up until now. Way more than enough.

No more.

She hadn't gone through the trauma of divorce and the sorrow of estrangement with her father to turn around and embrace more of the same from someone else.

So why was she fighting such a strong urge to

run and catch up to him? To grab him by the arm and tell him she was sorry he'd been so worried about her.

Why did her eyes suddenly sting and a painful lump form in her throat?

Because she was a fanciful nitwit who'd gone and developed feelings for a man who was utterly wrong for her. At a time when she shouldn't even be entertaining such a notion.

She'd been trying so hard to deny it. But she'd been unable to think of anything or anyone else since she'd woken up in his arms this morning.

The feel of his body wrapped around hers elicited emotions and longings she had no business feeling.

And all afternoon, her mind had replayed the hour in Lizzie's room when she'd drawn on his shoulder. The feel of his skin under her fingers. The woodsy, masculine scent of him mixed with the salty air he'd just been running in.

His surprised and bemused face when he'd realized what she'd tattooed on him. The butterfly had been a whim. He'd spoken of the butterfly effect that night before they'd traveled alone together down the Road to Hana to return the rock.

He hadn't made the connection. And why

should he? She'd obviously given it way too much thought. Spent too much time analyzing what would have happened if she'd never walked into that lounge at the airport. Or if he'd flown down in a private aircraft as per his usual routine. So many variables could have been even slightly altered and they would never have even crossed paths until the first wedding excursion. He most likely wouldn't have given her a second glance.

The same way he hadn't all those years ago when she'd first met him as a college coed.

CHAPTER ELEVEN

THE BEACH CHAIR wasn't so bad. At least as comfortable as the couch in Clint's suite. But definitely not as comfortable as his bed. Not that Rita was going to allow herself to think about being in his bed right now. Spending the night there was absolutely not an option this time. Not after their little exchange this afternoon due to her cliff-jumping adventure. Her pride would not allow it.

This was just fine; it wasn't even that cold out here on the beach. Only when the wind blew really hard did it get a little chilly. She could deal with that. For the next few hours she would just lie here with a big beach towel wrapped around her until Tessa's text let her know she could return to their room.

This time, she'd made Tessa promise not to fall asleep and forget.

Who needed Clint Fallon? Certainly not her.

She clung to that thought as the temperature gradually dipped lower over the next hour and a half. Her patience wearing thin, she double-checked her phone in case she'd missed Tessa's message.

Nothing.

All right. That was it. Tessa would get a few more minutes tops. Half an hour at the most. Then she was going to her room whether the other woman liked it or not. At this point, she didn't even care if Rob was still in there with her. She was so tired and sleepy, she probably wouldn't even be able to stay awake long enough to witness anything.

Somehow, despite the chattering of her teeth, she managed to doze off. She wasn't even sure how much time had gone by when a set of strong, warm arms suddenly reached around her middle. She felt herself being hoisted up, then nestled against a hard, blessedly warm chest. She immediately recognized his scent, even through the haze of groggy slumber.

Clint. Of course. "Hey."

"Hi, sweetheart."

"How did you find me?"

"I checked the lounge area but you weren't there. Then I just knew."

"You did?"

He shrugged, lifting her slightly higher and tighter against him. "Yeah, I don't really know how to explain it. It was like something led me directly to where you were."

"Huh."

"I know it's hard to believe."

Rita recalled the night after she'd picked up the rock. The eerie sensation that someone, or something, was there with her in that room. Trying to tell her something almost. How her shorts had ended up on the floor outside her closet. "I do believe you," she told him.

She leaned into his chest and snuggled further into his welcome warmth.

"Babe, I'm sorry." Clint spoke in her ear, his hot breath warming her cheek. "I want to kick myself that you felt the need to sleep out here."

"I wasn't going to all night. I was going to demand the use of my bed in just a few minutes. As soon as Tessa and Rob are finished." She stifled a giggle, not even sure what she was amused by. Now she was just downright giddy.

"You don't need to do that."

What was he referring to? Between being so cold and half-asleep, it was so hard to focus. "Do what?"

"Demand the use of your bed. You'll be sleeping in mine."

The whole first floor of the resort was deserted when they walked through. Before she knew it, they were somehow in Clint's suite and he was gently depositing her on the bed. She snuggled deep into the soft pillow as he tucked the covers around her.

"I'm sorry," she whispered into the darkness. "For earlier. For scaring you."

"Oh, sweetheart. I should have handled it better."

"You were angry."

She sensed more than saw him shaking his head. "It was more that I was scared."

Something had been nagging at her all evening. She should have thought about Clint's history, the way he'd lost his parents. She felt like a selfish, inconsiderate brat. No wonder he'd been so upset. "Your mom and dad died in a boating accident, didn't they?"

He blew out a breath. "Yeah, they were vacationing off the coast of Greece. Got caught in an unpredicted Mediterranean squall." He flinched as he softly recounted the memories. "They were always off somewhere, exploring the world. Just the two of them."

While their two children were foisted on a grandmother who didn't want them around, Rita thought. Only to be stuck with them permanently when tragedy hit.

"And one day they left and never returned."

"I'm so sorry you and Lizzie had to endure that."

He rubbed a hand down his face. "Ironically, that was the year Lizzie had a starring role in the middle school play. She'd begged them not to go."

Rita felt a surge of tenderness for her friend. The loss of her mother and father at such a critical age must have been unbearable. And what of poor Clint? In many ways, being the older sibling, he had it so much harder. Her heart ached for the young man he must have been. A young man suddenly stranded with more responsibility than he could have dreamed. And he'd accepted it with grace and dignity.

"Lizzie mentioned what happened two or three times while we were at school," she told him. "I didn't push for details. I got the impression she didn't really like talking about it."

"She doesn't. And I can't say as I blame her.

We both had to deal with their loss and move on as best we could."

He made it sound so simple. Perhaps deep down, he really believed it actually was.

"The adults you and Lizzie have both turned into despite all that is beyond impressive. Commendable."

"Thank you for saying that, sweet Rita."

Suddenly, Clint stood and turned to go.

She didn't want him to. "Clint, wait."

"Yeah?"

"Where are you going?"

He leaned over her to brush a loose strand of hair off her forehead, let his hand linger at her temple. "I'll go sleep on the couch. You know, in the interest of harmony."

She took his hand in hers before he could pull it away. "Stay."

It was the perfect day and setting for a wedding.

Rita followed the rest of the bridal procession to an archway covered in gorgeous tropical flowers on the beach. A small band behind them consisting of ukuleles and various drums played an island version of the wedding theme. All in all, the scene could have been out of a bridal magazine.

Or a young girl's fantasy. When they reached the front, the groomsmen broke off to one side, while she and the other bridesmaids went to stand opposite.

Then Clint walked out with his sister from a covered canopy, leading her down the aisle. Rita had to remind herself to breathe. She hadn't seen Clint since this morning when they'd woken up in each other's arms again after having easily fallen asleep together the night before. Then the hectic pace of wedding preparation had immediately taken hold of them all. Now looking at him in a formfitting tux with a Hawaiian flower in the lapel, she almost felt light-headed.

He had to be the most handsome, alluring man she'd ever known. And she'd have to say goodbye to him in about forty-eight hours.

Rita swallowed down the lump of sadness that settled in her throat. All fantasies came to an end. There was no use in wallowing. Served her right for letting her guard down and falling for a man who wanted nothing but freedom. On the heels of a failed marriage no less. Well, it seemed to follow a pattern of awful timing she'd somehow fallen into. Her first goal upon returning home would have to be to break out of it.

Lizzie beamed as she approached her groom, her smile as bright as the glowing Hawaiian sun above. Her dress was a delicate lacy piece that seemed to float around her as she walked. A tiara of beautiful flowers adorned her head and framed her angelic face. When they reached the archway, Clint gave his sister a soft peck on the cheek before putting her hand into Jonathon's outstretched one. As he walked toward the other groomsmen, he looked up to catch Rita's eye. The depth of emotion she saw in his gaze almost made her knees buckle.

How in the world was she supposed to go back to any semblance of a normal life after this? How was she supposed to live day to day as if none of this happened? While thinking of him every moment? For she had no doubt she'd be doing just that.

She'd gone and fallen in love with him. Who knew, perhaps it had been years in the making, since she'd first laid eyes on the man all those years ago. Now, with all the time they'd spent together in such close quarters, her feelings had developed into so much more.

She hadn't given him an answer. They still had two more days on Maui. To his credit, Clint hadn't even brought up the proposition he'd so casually made the other day. But she hadn't forgotten. She had no doubt he hadn't forgotten either. The rest of the ceremony seemed to go by in a daze.

She watched Clint clap as the officiator finally pronounced Lizzie and Jonathon man and wife. He'd done so well by his sister, Rita thought. From a young age he'd taken care of her, made sure she prospered and thrived. Now he'd given her the most dreamlike wedding.

He was sure to make his own bride a very lucky lady one day. Though he swore he wanted to remain single, there was no question that someday someone would come along who refused to let him go. A wise, clever woman would make it her life's goal to figure out how to snare him for good. Rita couldn't help but envy her.

In the meantime, did she have it in her to take the little he was willing to give?

"May I have the honor of this dance?"

Rita looked up to find Clint holding out his arm to her as she sat watching the bride and groom canoodling at the head table. The reception was in full swing now. Even random strangers walking along the beach had joined in the revelry. A couple of local residents were doing an impressive luau dance, their hips moving so fast it made Rita's pelvis hurt just watching them.

Taking Clint's hand, she followed him out to the dance floor. As if by fate, the bouncy rhythmic reggae number that had been playing suddenly switched to a slow Hawaiian love song.

Clint took her gently by the waist and pulled her tight against him. A curl of heat unwound deep in her belly and moved in every which direction.

"Hard to believe they're finally married," she offered by way of conversation.

He laughed against her cheek. "I was really worried for a while there that it might not happen."

"I always had faith," she countered. "In those two and in the spirits."

"Is that so?"

"Mmm-hmm. I knew the spirits wouldn't let us down." Not when it came to the wedding anyway. As far as her heart, the spirits had apparently decided she was on her own. It had been slowly breaking since she'd run into Clint back on the mainland.

She nodded against his neck, resisted the urge

to nestle closer and inhale deeply of his scent. She wouldn't be able to enjoy it much longer.

She pulled back to look him in the eye. "Clint, I haven't forgotten what you asked me."

He merely nodded, waiting for her to continue.

"I know I haven't given you an answer yet. I'm not sure that I can, even after all this time."

"Which is in itself answer enough, isn't it?"

Rita swallowed past the painful lump that suddenly formed at the base of her throat. This was so much harder than she'd expected. The truth was, she just couldn't do it, she couldn't have a casual affair. Not with him. Her heart was already lost to Clint Fallon. She couldn't bear to turn her soul over to him, as well. For that's what accepting his offer would do. She would never recover afterward, not when she had to walk away from him as if none of it mattered.

For several quiet moments, they just held each other, swaying softly to the music. Rita didn't trust herself to speak.

"So what's next for you, Sarita Paul?" he surprised her by asking. "Once we all return to reality, I mean."

"I guess I've got a lot to figure out."

"Well, if you're ever in the area," he said against her cheek. "You know the rest."

Something broke in the vicinity of her heart, an actual sensation of snapping that had her struggling for breath. How could he be so casual, so matter-of-fact about whether he would ever see her again? She had to get away before she made a fool of herself by sobbing into his chest.

She slipped out of his grasp and ran toward the crashing waves of the water. It didn't surprise her when his footsteps sounded in the sand behind her seconds later.

"Rita." He spoke her name softly, like a whisper on the wind.

"I'd like to be alone for a while."

"There are some things we should discuss, don't you think?"

She didn't dare turn to face him, afraid of what her face might give away. "Like what? Like how I should look you up when I'm in town? Is that what you'd like to discuss?" she asked over her shoulder.

It was no use. He came to clasp her by the shoulders and turned her to face him.

"You have a lot to figure out. You said so yourself. It would be selfish of me to stand in the way of that."

"Don't pretend that's why you're doing this, Clint. Please give me more credit than that."

He blinked at her.

"Why would you say that?" He seemed genuinely perplexed. For such a smart, accomplished man, he really could be very obtuse. Or he was working really hard at it.

"You're letting yourself off the hook by pretending this is all about me."

He let go of her shoulders and shoved his hands into his pockets. The action had the effect of pulling his shirt tight against the toned muscles of his chest and widening the V at his collar where he'd undone two buttons. The overall look was so devilishly handsome, she wanted nothing more than to forget this conversation and fling herself into his arms.

But that would only serve to prolong the inevitable.

"It's really more about you. And how scared you are."

He didn't meet her gaze, stared at the sand beneath their feet. "What exactly do you think I'm so afraid of, Rita? Please enlighten me."

She ignored the snark in his tone. "Of loving someone and then losing them. It's why you strive so hard to control what's around you. Who's around you. But you can't control human beings, Clint. Nor their feelings."

He looked up, off to the horizon and the setting sun behind her. His next words proved she was right about everything she'd just said.

"You may have a point. It doesn't change anything."

"How can you say that?" she pleaded, hating the sobbing quality of her voice.

"I was clear from the beginning, sweetheart. This was one week on an exotic tropical island. Reality is what it is."

The breaking in her chest she'd felt earlier turned into a violent shatter. "So that's it then? You're going to let fear and uncertainty keep you from moving forward? You're so ready to just turn your back on any feelings that you may find inconvenient."

His eyes narrowed on her face. "And what about you, Rita?"

"What about me?"

"You're not exactly in a position to cast stones."

What was he talking about? She wasn't the one ready to walk away from what they were beginning to feel for each other. Feelings she knew he had to be experiencing also. Or else what did that say about her?

"I have no idea what you mean."

"You really don't see it?"

"See what?"

"Let me ask you something. Exactly how have you moved forward since your divorce?"

What did Jay or her divorce have to do with anything? "What are you insinuating? Maybe you should just come out and say it."

He bit out a curse. "Fine. You're stuck in a holding pattern. Too afraid to move, too afraid to risk another chance at letting others down."

She sucked in some much-needed air. "You have no idea what you're saying. You don't know what it took to sever my marriage, the pain and anguish it caused me and to those around me."

"You're right. It did take a lot of courage. So now what?"

Rita wanted to slam her hands up against her ears. Suddenly, this conversation had turned into one about her. And all her shortcomings as far as Clint was concerned.

The way he saw her was breaking her heart.

He didn't wait for a response. Shaking his head, he continued, "You said you'd thought years ago about opening your own practice. Or maybe working for an animal shelter. Yet you plan on looking for another small office to join when you return. How is that any different than what you were originally trying to get away from?"

"It's very different."

He shrugged. "Is it? Perhaps. I guess I wouldn't know. But it's not what you really want."

"I'm trying to figure out what I want."

"So you say."

She willed the tears that now stung her eyes to keep from falling. He thought she was indecisive and weak. It hurt more than she would have thought.

"And what about your father?" he demanded to know.

"What about him?"

"You've stood up to him. And your relationship suffered. What are you going to do about it now?"

"We just need time," she cried out.

"And it will all miraculously work itself out?" he said with a questioning shrug. "Face it. You're stuck and it's because you've chosen to be. Both in terms of your career and your relationships."

"You have no idea what you're saying."

"I think I do. It's like you've made the climb up onto that cliff. But you're still just standing there, not ready to jump but not willing to climb back down."

So that's how he really saw her. The revelation felt like a physical blow. Lifting her chin, she summoned her voice despite the pain, despite the anger. "At least I made the climb, Clint. Look around you and see if you can say the same."

Something shifted behind his eyes; they suddenly grew darker. She thought he started to reach for her, but it was too late. Rita stepped away and strode past him as far as she could before she had to catch her breath. Maybe it made her a coward but she had to flee. Before he could hurt her anymore.

Clint glanced at his watch and scanned the outdoor reception area once more. There was no sign of her. She'd stormed away from him about two hours ago. And now it was almost midnight and he hadn't seen her since.

He'd already checked her room and tried calling her repeatedly. Man, he really shouldn't have gone off on her like that. Now that he'd cooled down, he figured he should find her and try to apologize. But she was nowhere to be found.

As much as he didn't want to worry his sister on her wedding night, he was going to have to ask her if she knew where Rita was. Either that or he was ready to call the authorities and round up a search party.

He approached Lizzie where she stood by a buffet table feeding Jonathon various pieces of fruit.

"Hey, sis, got a sec?"

"For my big brother? Always."

"You're leaving me here alone?" Jonathon petulantly asked. "It's our wedding night. I thought we might retire soon."

Lizzie gave him a hard kiss on the lips. "I won't be long. You wait right here for me."

Clint bit down on the nausea that little exchange invoked and pulled his sister to the side.

"Sorry for the interruption. And I don't want to worry you, but I haven't seen Rita in several hours. She's not answering her phone. Have you heard from her?"

Lizzie's smile faded and her face fell. "Oh, Clint. You don't know?"

A bad feeling started to bloom in his chest. "Know what?"

"Rita decided she'd been away from home too long. Asked if I'd mind if she left a couple days early."

"She's gone?"

Lizzie nodded; lines of sympathy etched her eyes. "Now that the reception is over, I told her it was fine. Apparently, there are some pressing matters she needs to address back home. She's taking the red-eye out. You two didn't discuss it?"

He could only shake his head.

"I'm surprised she didn't say anything to you."

"Not a thing." Not directly anyway. Indirectly, she'd told him everything he needed to know. And then she'd just up and left. Without so much as a word of goodbye.

Well, what did he expect? After the way he'd confronted her earlier, she would have had every right to slap him before storming off. And he would have deserved it.

"I'm sorry, big brother." He could barely hear Lizzie over the sudden roaring in his ears. "If I'd realized you didn't know, I would have come to find you right away."

Rita was gone. "It's not your fault. You should get back to your groom."

"What about you?"

He shrugged. "I'll be fine, just need some salty air." Turning, Clint made his way toward the beach, toward the spot he'd stood arguing with Rita. Was that the last spot he would ever see her? The notion sent a painful stab in the area of his chest.

Lizzie was following him. He turned around to give her a questioning look. They'd reached the beach.

"What happened between you two?"

"Nothing you need to concern yourself with. Not now of all times. You just got married for heaven's sake."

"That may be so. But I'll always have time for my big brother."

Clint forced a smile and crouched down in front of the crashing waves. To his surprise, Lizzie dropped down next to him, sitting right on her bottom in the sand. She pulled her wedding dress tighter around her as a small gust of wind carried over from the water.

"I've known Rita for years," she began. "She's one in a million. Whatever went wrong, I'm guessing it was completely the result of you being your usual foolhardy and rigid self."

His sister could be quite blunt. "My only defense is I never tried to lead her to believe otherwise."

"I see. And you think that absolves you somehow?"

He rubbed a hand down his face. "I don't know what I think," he answered truthfully. "This was all supposed to be so simple, so straightforward."

"And all within your control."

He gave her a side-eye glare. "Don't start, Lizzie. I don't want to fight with you too."

"So, you two did have a fight then."

Could it even be called that? Apparently, he and Rita had both been making all sorts of observations about each other. While failing to look within themselves. "More of a heated discussion. Rita felt compelled to point out a few things that she thought I was missing. About my behavior. I sort of returned the salvo."

"I see. What did Rita have to say?"

"I'm sure you can guess."

"That you insist on taking charge because you think if you control as many circumstances as you can, you can spare yourself?"

"Did you two compare notes?"

"You're not exactly an enigma, big brother."

He humphed at that.

She remained silent for a while, played with the sand around her. When she spoke again, the change in topic threw him for a loop. "Jonathon and I decided we'd like a very big family. Like his. And we want to start right away."

Clint didn't bother to stifle his groan. Hadn't he been through enough tonight? "Is that your very uncouth way of telling me that you're going back to your groom now?"

She laughed. "No, I just want you to think about what that means. For you in particular."

"For me?" Where in the world could she possibly be going with this. He honestly had no clue.

"When you become an uncle. Are you going to avoid my children? For fear of growing too affectionate of them?"

"Of course not, especially if they're lucky enough to resemble their uncle."

"Ha ha. The simple truth is that you'll love them and cherish them from the moment they arrive in this world until your very last day. That's just who you are."

"Of course, I will." What was the point of this

conversation she was leading him down? Now of all times. And here of all places, on the beach after her wedding.

"And what about me? Did you ever think it'd be easier just to write me off when I became an adult? You never stopped caring about me."

"Are you getting to some kind of point? You're my sister. Your children will be my nieces and nephews. How in the world would I have any choice in the matter when it came to loving them or caring about them? Or you?"

She actually had the gall to throw sand in his direction. He closed his eyes just in time but couldn't avoid several grains landing directly into his mouth.

"You have no clue, do you?"

Clint made an exaggerated show of spitting out the offending sand. "About what?"

"Don't be dense. From where I'm standing, it's patently clear that you have no choice when it comes to Rita either."

Rita pulled out her boarding pass and reconfirmed her seat as she made it to the sitting area of terminal twenty at Kahului Airport. To think, just a few short days ago she'd been in a different airport ready to board a different flight, completely unaware that she was about to come face-to-face with the man she would fall in love with.

For that's exactly what had happened. She could no longer deny it. She'd fallen head over heels for Clint Fallon. But she couldn't manage to figure out a way to reach him. Hard to believe, but this was so much worse than her marriage failing. Her divorce had led to feelings of sadness and profound failure.

When it came to Clint, she felt absolute, sharp, nearly unbearable pain.

Biting back tears, she made her way to one of the many empty chairs to wait for boarding. What was Clint doing at this very moment? Had he even noticed she'd gone?

She felt a small twinge of guilt about leaving him back there without so much as a word. But what was there left to say?

You've made the climb up onto that cliff. But you're still just standing there...

His words were so unkind. So unfair.

She'd taken a giant leap by insisting on splitting from Jay. Hadn't she? Of course she had. Look at the ramifications it had led to, the hit her relationship with her father had taken.

And what had she done about that? Nothing so far. As Clint had made sure to point out.

Without giving herself time to think, she pulled her phone out of her pocket and called up her parents' number. What time was it on the East Coast? Early morning, but she didn't care. Not right now.

Her mother picked up on the second ring. "Rita, is everything all right? It's awfully early."

"I'm sorry. I just wanted to talk to Dad. Is he up?"

"You know he is. He always wakes up at the crack of dawn. What's this about, dear? Are you sure everything's all right?"

No, she wanted to wail out. And it would never be all right again. "Yes, Ma. I promise."

Her mother hesitated a few moments before Rita heard shuffling on the other end of the line. Seconds later, her father's rich baritone and mild accent greeted her with concern.

"Sarita? What's this about? Do you need help? Where are you?"

The concern in his voice brought tears to her eyes. She knew he cared about her; he loved her deeply. But it was no longer enough. She wanted more from him. And she was ready to ask for it.

"Everything's fine, Pa. I just wanted to tell you that I love you."

Dead air. Finally, her father cleared his throat. "I...love you too, sweetheart. You have me quite concerned though, dear one. Do you need to be picked up?"

Rita swallowed down the lump in her throat and forced herself to keep talking. "No, I'm fine. I just need you to talk to me. To be my father."

"I don't understand."

No, he didn't. But she would do everything in her power to make him understand. "And I want you to be proud to be my father. But it can't be solely on your terms, Papa."

Then she could no longer hold the tears back at all.

CHAPTER TWELVE

IF RITA CLOSED her eyes and concentrated long enough, she could easily imagine she was back in Hawaii sitting in a lounge chair on the beach. She could almost feel the salty air against her face and the sun shining bright and hot, warming up her skin.

Hard to believe it was only two weeks since she'd returned. Rather than a sandy beach, she was sitting behind a desk trying to put the final pieces in place to kick off the annual fund-raiser for the Greater Westport Animal Shelter. Not that she was complaining. Somehow, she'd landed her dream job within days of getting back from Lizzie and Jonathon's wedding. Who was she kidding? If it wasn't for Clint and the way he'd confronted her about moving forward with her life, she would have never had the gumption to apply for it.

Even her father was impressed. He'd actually taken her out to lunch to celebrate when she'd told her parents the news last week. Rita's eyes stung as she recalled her father's efforts that afternoon. They'd never, ever sat down together one-on-one just to talk. He'd actually said he was proud of her and her newfound position. She couldn't have been more surprised if he'd jumped on the diner counter and started doing a step dance.

His words echoed in her head still. *You've always had the sheer will and strength to go after what you wanted.*

There was at least one exception, Rita thought. Those qualities her father touted had failed her perhaps when it mattered the most. And she would have to live with that for the rest of her life.

Thank goodness for how demanding the new job was. It was keeping her just busy enough that memories of Clint Fallon only plagued her at night. Except for those moments during the day when a pair of dark brown eyes flashed in her vision, or she thought she smelled the woodsy scent of Clint's aftershave.

Rita threw her pen down on the desk in disgust. Who was she kidding? Hardly a moment went by that he wasn't in her thoughts. Every time her cell rang, her heart leaped to her throat. Until she saw on the screen who it was. Never him.

So far she'd resisted the urge to call her friend under the pretense of asking about her newly married life just to get info on her brother.

But she wouldn't allow herself to stoop to that level.

A sudden knock on the door was followed by her vet technician popping her head in. "I'm really sorry about the interruption, Dr. Paul. But there's a man out here who insists he needs to see you before he'll sign off on his adoption. Refuses to speak with anyone else."

Rita looked up from the paperwork she'd been shuffling. She had to get through it all so that she could start her rounds with the animals. But it had been hard to focus.

"I'd ask him to leave," Val continued. "But he seems really interested in one of the pups. I'd hate for the little fella to miss a chance at adoption."

"That doesn't explain why he needs to see me specifically."

"Should I get Frank from the auto parts shop next door to show him out?" Val asked.

Rita let out a long sigh. Looked like the paperwork and the animals were going to have to wait a little longer. "No, it's okay. I'll talk to him. Thanks."

She did a double take when the visitor entered the room.

Rita rubbed her eyes. Maybe this wasn't real. Maybe she was simply seeing what she wanted to see. But then he spoke. And all doubt fled. Her heart fluttered like a hummingbird in her chest.

"Hey, remember me?"

"Clint?"

"Hi, sweetheart."

"What are you doing here?"

He shrugged, shut the door behind him as Val stepped away. Rita thought she heard the younger woman giggle. "I wanted to show you something."

This was surreal. All this time she'd been willing the phone to ring. Just to be able to hear his voice would have sent her soaring with happiness. But here he was. In the flesh.

She wasn't sure how her mouth was working but somehow she managed to speak. "Show me what?"

Her jaw dropped when he started unbuttoning his shirt, then shrugged it off. Suddenly, Clint Fallon was standing in her newly gained office, shirtless and smiling. How many surprises could she be dealt today?

"My tattoo," he answered her.

Turning, he pointed to his back above the shoulder blade. Rita's vision clouded as she realized what she was looking at. He'd gone and made her butterfly permanent after all. "I had the tattoo artist trace your design before it could fade."

"Oh, Clint." Without thinking, she flung out of her chair and into his embrace. His strong arms went immediately around her. He smelled the same.

"Does that mean you like it?"

She couldn't summon the words to express what she felt.

"I haven't stopped thinking about you," he whispered as he dropped devastating kisses along her temple, down her cheek. Then he took her lips brutally with his. Rita felt the kiss down to her core. "I missed you."

She pulled away. "Oh, Clint. I missed you too. What took you so long?"

"I wanted to make sure to give you enough time, then I couldn't wait any longer. I've barely been functioning these past few weeks." He paused to look around her office. "Whereas you've clearly been busy. I read about your new post online. Congratulations, babe."

She sniffled. "It was a long shot. I didn't think I was qualified for the director position, of all things."

"Oh, Rita."

"But then I thought about what you said. About just jumping off the rock cliff."

"I'm sorry about that night. I'm so sorry I said all those things."

She hugged him tighter. "Please don't apologize. I needed to hear it all. I needed to hear it from you."

He sniffed her hair. "But I should have also told you how extraordinary I think you are."

"You do?"

"Oh, babe. You're warm, witty, generous. You make sure a wandering dog isn't a stray and that it's well taken care of. You're a staunchly loyal friend. You don't think twice about driving up a harrowing mountain to return a rock which may be jinxing your friend's wedding, just in case it's real."

She had to chuckle at that. "Some men might call that feckless and silly."

"Not this man." He shuddered in her arms. "But please don't try anything like that again. Not without me."

He had no idea. She didn't want to do much of anything these days without him by her side.

"I won't. And as far as loyalty, you have it in spades yourself, Mr. Fallon."

"Huh?" he studied her.

"Oh, Clint. Don't you know how impressive it is? The way you made sure to not only take care of your sister from such a young age but also to help her thrive. And look at all you've accomplished. Completely on your own. I've been in awe of you since the day I met you at school move-in day." She inhaled deeply, decided to make yet another jump. "And now, after all these years, I've gone and fallen in love with you."

He actually lifted her off the ground. Did a mini spin. "Well, that happens to work out, Dr. Paul. Because I've fallen madly, irreversibly in love with you too. We should really do something about that."

He took her lips once more, delved deeply into her mouth. Rita had to catch her breath when he finally pulled away.

"You love me?"

"As sure as the sun rises over that freezing-cold crater every morning."

Rita was certain her heart had burst in her chest. This was beyond any fantasy she'd dreamed up.

"Oh, by the way, I plan on adopting that poor, ridiculously tiny Chihuahua out there."

She couldn't help but laugh. "The Chihuahua? Really? I would have pegged you for a…larger, more rugged breed."

He shrugged and flashed her a smile that sent heat simmering over her skin. "What can I say? You don't seem to have any of those hairless cats."

"They're called Sphynx cats," she reminded him.

"Whatever. The little fella called to me. Plus, your staff told me that he's been here the longest."

A wealth of emotion flooded her chest and threatened to split her heart open. She was completely, steadfastly, head over heels in love with this man. Perhaps she'd loved him since she'd first laid eyes on him as a young college student. Back then, he had seemed beyond her reach, someone to dream about. Now, all these years later, here he was, making her dreams a reality.

"Then he's yours," she vowed, laughing some more when he picked her up and sat her on the desk. "I shall personally vouch for you."

"Good. Guess what?"

"What?"

"You're mine too."

EPILOGUE

One year later

"YOU KNOW, it's our anniversary too," Clint informed her as he turned onto the roadway leading to Wai'anapanapa State Park.

"Is that so?"

"You bet. It was exactly one year ago that I kissed you for the first time. I don't suppose you remember."

Rita waited for him to park and got out of the car before she answered. "I remember everything about that trip." The statement earned her a deep kiss that had her toes curling. The effect Clint had on her senses had not diminished in the slightest in the year since they'd been on this island for Lizzie's wedding. They'd joined the couple here for a celebratory trip in honor of their first anniversary. Never would Rita have guessed back then that she'd be here with Clint for such an occasion a year later.

A strange sense of déjà vu overcame her as they walked down the steps leading to Black Sand Beach. It was hard not to feel slightly silly when she thought about the superstitious reason behind the need she'd felt to return a silly rock. Superstition could be a powerful thing, it turned out.

Clint held her hand as they made it to the bottom. The waves were quieter today than that morning a year ago. The dark sand was the color of black onyx, just as she remembered. They walked farther toward the water. Though he hadn't come out and said so, Rita knew where he was taking her, touched that he'd thought to do so. He'd obviously been planning.

There it was. The cave where she'd first touched him, where she'd first asked him to kiss her.

"Do you think you'd recognize it?" he asked in a light, teasing voice. "Your rock?"

"I have no doubt. It was a very special one that called to me."

They stepped inside the opening and immediately all the warm memories came flooding back. She wrapped her arms around his neck and gave in to the desire to kiss him.

"I, for one, am glad you picked it up all those

months ago," Clint said against her mouth. "Or else I would have never gotten you in here alone."

"Very true."

He winked at her. "See if you can find it."

He was serious. "That's ridiculous, Clint. It was a year ago. It's probably nowhere near here anymore."

"It was magical, remember? Look around. You never know."

Rita let out a resigned groan. Just to humor him, she looked down along the ground, then stood upright. "It's not here."

Clint shook his head. "You didn't even try. Look again. At exactly the spot you left it last year."

Why was he doing this? All she wanted to do was enjoy the scenery and then go indulge in some of that delicious banana bread she'd been thinking about all day.

"If you insist."

Stooping lower, she searched the spot where she remembered dropping the rock so many months ago. Not that she really knew for sure what to look for. All the rocks looked exactly the same.

A small speck of white caught her eye on the ground near the cave wall. She bent to pick it up.

"What is that?" Clint asked, taking her hand to study it.

"A flower. Or half of one. How'd a broken flower get in a beachside cave?"

Clint shrugged. "It doesn't appear to be any old flower."

Rita looked closer. He was right. Upon closer inspection, it appeared the flower hadn't been torn in half at all. "It looks like it somehow bloomed that way, only half a flower. I've never seen anything like it."

"It's beautiful. You know, now that I think about it, I've heard about these flowers. They're native to Hawaii."

"You have?"

"Yes. It's coming back to me. The story behind it. It's called a *naupaka* flower."

Rita narrowed her gaze on his face. Something was up. Clint wasn't normally the type to pay attention to legends or stories. Even if he had indulged her last year when she'd felt the urgent need to return a displaced pebble. And he certainly wasn't the type to remember the name of a flower.

"What's this story?" she asked him.

"More a legend really. About a princess."

"Another sad story about a princess?"

Clint pursed his lips and nodded. "I'm afraid so. Apparently, she fell in love with a man who was already spoken for. He felt the same way about her but the gods decreed they were not meant to be. Since she couldn't give him her heart, she took a flower from her hair and tore it in half. Until their deaths, they each carried half the flower with them always. It's been blooming that way ever since."

Rita didn't know quite what to say. It really was a beautiful, touching story. But it still didn't explain how the flower had gotten here. Or why Clint knew so much about it.

He continued with the rest of the legend. "It's said that when the two halves of the flower find each other, then true love blossoms."

He hadn't finished uttering the last word when Clint suddenly bent down on his knee before her. Reaching in his pocket, he pulled out two items. One a small velvet box.

The world spun around her head. She forgot to breathe.

And then she realized what the other item he held was—the other half of the flower. He must have been planning this for so long. All of it for her. Tears stung her eyes as she looked into the love that showed in his. How in the world had she gotten to be so fortunate?

"Sarita Ann Paul," he began. He took her hand and opened the box to reveal a breathtaking stone set in a glittering band. It was the most exquisite ring she'd ever seen.

"Would you do me the honor of marrying me?"

Rita barely heard him over the roaring in her ears and the overwhelming joy in her heart. As much as she'd dreamed, nothing could have prepared her for what was happening. Clint Fallon had just asked her to be his wife.

Somehow, she found her voice despite the flood of emotion pouring out of her soul. "Yes. A million times over. Yes!"

* * * * *

LET'S TALK
Romance

For exclusive extracts, competitions
and special offers, find us online:

f facebook.com/millsandboon

⊙ @millsandboonuk

𝕏 @millsandboon

Or get in touch on 0844 844 1351*

For all the latest titles coming soon,
visit millsandboon.co.uk/nextmonth

*Calls cost 7p per minute plus your phone company's price per
minute access charge

Want even more
ROMANCE?

Join our bookclub today!

'Mills & Boon books, the perfect way to escape for an hour or so.'

Miss W. Dyer

'Excellent service, promptly delivered and very good subscription choices.'

Miss A. Pearson

'You get fantastic special offers and the chance to get books before they hit the shops'

Mrs V. Hall

Visit millsandbook.co.uk/Bookclub and save on brand new books.

MILLS & BOON